DOVER·THRIFT·EDITIONS

Much Ado About Nothing

WILLIAM SHAKESPEARE

DOVER PUBLICATIONS, INC.
New York

Note

First performed in 1598, *Much Ado About Nothing* focuses on the love story of Claudio and Hero, but the volatile relationship between Beatrice and Benedick is much more compelling. Critic Dover Wilson calls Beatrice "the first woman in [English] literature . . . who not only has a brain, but delights in the constant employment of it." Her sharp wit leads her to wage a war of words with Benedick, supplying much of the comic energy of the play. But when Hero is cruelly wronged by Claudio, Beatrice's wit and intelligence cannot defend her cousin's reputation; outraged at such injustice, she can only exclaim, "O God, that I were a man!" and convince Benedick to challenge Claudio. Though the couples are united in a conventionally comic ending, *Much Ado About Nothing* goes much deeper in exploring the tensions between the sexes in a society where female chastity is equated with virtue, and that virtue serves as the measure of a woman's worth.

Performance

This Dover Thrift Edition may be used in its entirety, in adaptation or in any other way for theatrical productions, professional and amateur, in the United States, without fee, permission or acknowledgment. (This may not apply outside of the United States, as copyright conditions may vary.)

Bibliographical Note

This Dover edition, first published in 1994, is an unabridged republication of the text as it originally appeared in Volume II of the second edition of *The Works of William Shakespeare*, published by Macmillan and Co., London, 1891. An introductory Note and explanatory footnotes have been prepared specially for this edition.

Library of Congress Cataloging-in-Publication Data

Shakespeare, William, 1564–1616.
  Much Ado about nothing / William Shakespeare.
    p.   cm. — (Dover thrift editions)
  ISBN-13: 978-0-486-28272-5 (pbk.)
  ISBN-10: 0-486-28272-4 (pbk.)
  I. Title. II. Series.
PR2828.A2Z56 1994   94–22079
822.3'3 — dc20   CIP

Manufactured in the United States by Courier Corporation
28272415
www.doverpublications.com

Contents

Dramatis Personæ

DON PEDRO, prince of Arragon.
DON JOHN, his bastard brother.
CLAUDIO, a young lord of Florence.
BENEDICK, a young lord of Padua.
LEONATO, governor of Messina.
ANTONIO, his brother.
BALTHASAR, attendant on Don Pedro.
CONRADE, ⎫ followers of Don John.
BORACHIO, ⎭
FRIAR FRANCIS.
DOGBERRY, a constable.
VERGES, a headborough.[1]
A Sexton.
A Boy.

HERO, daughter to Leonato.
BEATRICE, niece to Leonato.
Margaret, ⎫ gentlewomen attending on Hero.
Ursula, ⎭

Messengers, Watch, Attendants, &c.

Scene — *Messina.*

---

1. *headborough*] a kind of village-mayor.

ACT I.

SCENE I. *Before* LEONATO'S *house*.

Enter LEONATO, HERO, *and* BEATRICE, *with a* Messenger.

LEON.   I learn in this letter that Don Pedro of Arragon comes this night to Messina.

MESS.   He is very near by this: he was not three leagues off when I left him.

LEON.   How many gentlemen have you lost in this action?

MESS.   But few of any sort, and none of name.

LEON.   A victory is twice itself when the achiever brings home full numbers. I find here that Don Pedro hath bestowed much honour on a young Florentine called Claudio.

MESS.   Much deserved on his part, and equally remembered by Don Pedro: he hath borne himself beyond the promise of his age; doing, in the figure of a lamb, the feats of a lion: he hath indeed better bettered expectation than you must expect of me to tell you how.

LEON.   He hath an uncle here in Messina will be very much glad of it.

MESS.   I have already delivered him letters, and there appears much joy in him; even so much, that joy could not show itself modest enough without a badge of bitterness.

LEON.   Did he break out into tears?

MESS.   In great measure.

LEON.   A kind overflow of kindness: there are no faces truer than those that are so washed. How much better is it to weep at joy than to joy at weeping!

BEAT.   I pray you, is Signior Mountanto[1] returned from the wars or no?

---

1. *Mountanto*] a fencing term for an upward thrust.

1

MESS. I know none of that name, lady: there was none such in the army of any sort.

LEON. What is he that you ask for, niece?

HERO. My cousin means Signior Benedick of Padua.

MESS. O, he's returned; and as pleasant as ever he was.

BEAT. He set up his bills here in Messina and challenged Cupid at the flight;[2] and my uncle's fool, reading the challenge, subscribed for Cupid, and challenged him at the bird-bolt.[3] I pray you, how many hath he killed and eaten in these wars? But how many hath he killed? for, indeed, I promised to eat all of his killing.

LEON. Faith, niece, you tax Signior Benedick too much; but he'll be meet with you, I doubt it not.

MESS. He hath done good service, lady, in these wars.

BEAT. You had musty victual, and he hath holp to eat it: he is a very valiant trencher-man;[4] he hath an excellent stomach.

MESS. And a good soldier too, lady.

BEAT. And a good soldier to a lady; but what is he to a lord?

MESS. A lord to a lord, a man to a man; stuffed with all honourable virtues.

BEAT. It is so, indeed; he is no less than a stuffed man: but for the stuffing,—well, we are all mortal.

LEON. You must not, sir, mistake my niece. There is a kind of merry war betwixt Signior Benedick and her: they never meet but there's a skirmish of wit between them.

BEAT. Alas! he gets nothing by that. In our last conflict four of his five wits[5] went halting off, and now is the whole man governed with one: so that if he have wit enough to keep himself warm, let him bear it for a difference between himself and his horse; for it is all the wealth that he hath left, to be known a reasonable creature. Who is his companion now? He hath every month a new sworn brother.

MESS. Is't possible?

---

2. *flight*] long-distance shooting.
3. *bird-bolt*] a short, blunt, stumpy arrow used for killing birds.
4. *trencher-man*] a trencher is a plate; Beatrice is making fun of Benedick's appetite.
5. *five wits*] distinguished from the five senses, the five wits were common wit, imagination, fantasy, judgment and memory.

BEAT.   Very easily possible: he wears his faith but as the fashion of his hat; it ever changes with the next block.

MESS.   I see, lady, the gentleman is not in your books.

BEAT.   No; an he were, I would burn my study. But, I pray you, who is his companion? Is there no young squarer[6] now that will make a voyage with him to the devil?

MESS.   He is most in the company of the right noble Claudio.

BEAT.   O Lord, he will hang upon him like a disease: he is sooner caught than the pestilence, and the taker runs presently mad. God help the noble Claudio! if he have caught the Benedick, it will cost him a thousand pound ere a' be cured.

MESS.   I will hold friends with you, lady.

BEAT.   Do, good friend.

LEON.   You will never run mad, niece.

BEAT.   No, not till a hot January.

MESS.   Don Pedro is approached.

Enter DON PEDRO, DON JOHN, CLAUDIO, BENEDICK, *and* BALTHASAR.

D. PEDRO.   Good Signior Leonato, you are come to meet your trouble: the fashion of the world is to avoid cost, and you encounter it.

LEON.   Never came trouble to my house in the likeness of your Grace: for trouble being gone, comfort should remain; but when you depart from me, sorrow abides, and happiness takes his leave.

D. PEDRO.   You embrace your charge too willingly. I think this is your daughter.

LEON.   Her mother hath many times told me so.

BENE.   Were you in doubt, sir, that you asked her?

LEON.   Signior Benedick, no; for then were you a child.

D. PEDRO.   You have it full, Benedick: we may guess by this what you are, being a man. Truly, the lady fathers herself. Be happy, lady; for you are like an honourable father.

BENE.   If Signior Leonato be her father, she would not have his head on her shoulders for all Messina, as like him as she is.

BEAT.   I wonder that you will still be talking, Signior Benedick: nobody marks you.

---

6. *squarer*] braggart.

BENE. What, my dear Lady Disdain! are you yet living?

BEAT. Is it possible disdain should die while she hath such meet food to feed it, as Signior Benedick? Courtesy itself must convert to disdain, if you come in her presence.

BENE. Then is courtesy a turncoat. But it is certain I am loved of all ladies, only you excepted: and I would I could find in my heart that I had not a hard heart; for, truly, I love none.

BEAT. A dear happiness to women: they would else have been troubled with a pernicious suitor. I thank God and my cold blood, I am of your humour for that: I had rather hear my dog bark at a crow than a man swear he loves me.

BENE. God keep your ladyship still in that mind! so some gentleman or other shall 'scape a predestinate scratched face.

BEAT. Scratching could not make it worse, an 'twere such a face as yours were.

BENE. Well, you are a rare parrot-teacher.

BEAT. A bird of my tongue is better than a beast of yours.

BENE. I would my horse had the speed of your tongue, and so good a continuer. But keep your way, i' God's name; I have done.

BEAT. You always end with a jade's trick: I know you of old.

D. PEDRO. That is the sum of all, Leonato. Signior Claudio and Signior Benedick, my dear friend Leonato hath invited you all. I tell him we shall stay here at the least a month; and he heartily prays some occasion may detain us longer. I dare swear he is no hypocrite, but prays from his heart.

LEON. If you swear, my lord, you shall not be forsworn. [*To* DON JOHN] Let me bid you welcome, my lord: being reconciled to the prince your brother, I owe you all duty.

D. JOHN. I thank you: I am not of many words, but I thank you.

LEON. Please it your Grace lead on?

D. PEDRO. Your hand, Leonato; we will go together.

[*Exeunt all except* BENEDICK *and* CLAUDIO.]

CLAUD. Benedick, didst thou note the daughter of Signior Leonato?

BENE. I noted her not; but I looked on her.

CLAUD. Is she not a modest young lady?

BENE. Do you question me, as an honest man should do, for my simple true judgement? or would you have me speak after my custom, as being a professed tyrant to their sex?

CLAUD. No; I pray thee speak in sober judgement.

BENE.   Why, i'faith, methinks she's too low for a high praise, too brown for a fair praise, and too little for a great praise: only this commendation I can afford her, that were she other than she is, she were unhandsome; and being no other but as she is, I do not like her.

CLAUD.   Thou thinkest I am in sport: I pray thee tell me truly how thou likest her.

BENE.   Would you buy her, that you inquire after her?

CLAUD.   Can the world buy such a jewel?

BENE.   Yea, and a case to put it into. But speak you this with a sad brow? or do you play the flouting Jack, to tell us Cupid is a good hare-finder,[7] and Vulcan a rare carpenter? Come, in what key shall a man take you, to go in the song?

CLAUD.   In mine eye she is the sweetest lady that ever I looked on.

BENE.   I can see yet without spectacles, and I see no such matter: there's her cousin, an she were not possessed with a fury, exceeds her as much in beauty as the first of May doth the last of December. But I hope you have no intent to turn husband, have you?

CLAUD.   I would scarce trust myself, though I had sworn the contrary, if Hero would be my wife.

BENE.   Is't come to this? In faith, hath not the world one man but he will wear his cap with suspicion? Shall I never see a bachelor of threescore again? Go to, i'faith; an thou wilt needs thrust thy neck into a yoke, wear the print of it, and sigh away Sundays. Look; Don Pedro is returned to seek you.

Re-enter DON PEDRO.

D. PEDRO.   What secret hath held you here, that you followed not to Leonato's?

BENE.   I would your Grace would constrain me to tell.

D. PEDRO.   I charge thee on thy allegiance.

BENE.   You hear, Count Claudio: I can be secret as a dumb man; I would have you think so; but, on my allegiance, mark you this, on my allegiance. He is in love. With who? now that is your Grace's part. Mark how short his answer is;—With Hero, Leonato's short daughter.

---

7. *hare-finder*] a director of a hare hunt, chosen for his keen vision.

CLAUD.   If this were so, so were it uttered.

BENE.   Like the old tale, my lord: 'it is not so, nor 'twas not so, but, indeed, God forbid it should be so.'

CLAUD.   If my passion change not shortly, God forbid it should be otherwise.

D. PEDRO.   Amen, if you love her; for the lady is very well worthy.

CLAUD.   You speak this to fetch me in, my lord.

D. PEDRO.   By my troth, I speak my thought.

CLAUD.   And, in faith, my lord, I spoke mine.

BENE.   And, by my two faiths and troths, my lord, I spoke mine.

CLAUD.   That I love her, I feel.

D. PEDRO.   That she is worthy, I know.

BENE.   That I neither feel how she should be loved, nor know how she should be worthy, is the opinion that fire cannot melt out of me: I will die in it at the stake.

D. PEDRO.   Thou wast ever an obstinate heretic in the despite of beauty.

CLAUD.   And never could maintain his part but in the force of his will.

BENE.   That a woman conceived me, I thank her; that she brought me up, I likewise give her most humble thanks: but that I will have a recheat winded in my forehead,[8] or hang my bugle in an invisible baldrick,[9] all women shall pardon me. Because I will not do them the wrong to mistrust any, I will do myself the right to trust none; and the fine is, for the which I may go the finer, I will live a bachelor.

D. PEDRO.   I shall see thee, ere I die, look pale with love.

BENE.   With anger, with sickness, or with hunger, my lord; not with love: prove that ever I lose more blood with love than I will get again with drinking, pick out mine eyes with a ballad-maker's pen, and hang me up at the door of a brothel-house for the sign of blind Cupid.

D. PEDRO.   Well, if ever thou dost fall from this faith, thou wilt prove a notable argument.

---

8. *a recheat . . . forehead*] to "wind a recheat" is to sound a note on the huntsman's bugle; Benedick refers to the popular notion that horns sprout from the forehead of a cuckolded husband.

9. *baldrick*] the belt in which the huntsman's bugle is carried.

BENE.   If I do, hang me in a bottle like a cat, and shoot at me; and he that hits me, let him be clapped on the shoulder and called Adam.[10]

D. PEDRO.   Well, as time shall try:
          'In time the savage bull doth bear the yoke.'

BENE.   The savage bull may; but if ever the sensible Benedick bear it, pluck off the bull's horns, and set them in my forehead: and let me be vilely painted; and in such great letters as they write 'Here is good horse to hire,' let them signify under my sign 'Here you may see Benedick the married man.'

CLAUD.   If this should ever happen, thou wouldst be horn-mad.

D. PEDRO.   Nay, if Cupid have not spent all his quiver in Venice, thou wilt quake for this shortly.

BENE.   I look for an earthquake too, then.

D. PEDRO.   Well, you will temporize with the hours. In the meantime, good Signior Benedick, repair to Leonato's: commend me to him, and tell him I will not fail him at supper; for indeed he hath made great preparation.

BENE.   I have almost matter enough in me for such an embassage; and so I commit you—

CLAUD.   To the tuition of God: From my house, if I had it,—

D. PEDRO.   The sixth of July:[11] Your loving friend, Benedick.

BENE.   Nay, mock not, mock not. The body of your discourse is sometime guarded with fragments, and the guards are but slightly basted on neither: ere you flout old ends any further, examine your conscience: and so I leave you.   [*Exit.*]

CLAUD.   My liege, your highness now may do me good.

D. PEDRO.   My love is thine to teach: teach it but how,
          And thou shalt see how apt it is to learn
          Any hard lesson that may do thee good.

CLAUD.   Hath Leonato any son, my lord?

D. PEDRO.   No child but Hero; she's his only heir.

---

10. *hang me ... Adam*] shooting at a cat enclosed in a wooden bottle or barrel was a favorite country sport; "Adam" may be a reference to Adam Bell, the outlaw of ballad tradition, held to be a champion archer.

11. *The sixth of July*] Midsummer-day according to older calculations; a fit date for midsummer madness.

Dost thou affect her, Claudio?
CLAUD.   O, my lord,
    When you went onward on this ended action,
    I look'd upon her with a soldier's eye,
    That liked, but had a rougher task in hand
    Than to drive liking to the name of love:
    But now I am return'd and that war-thoughts
    Have left their places vacant, in their rooms
    Come thronging soft and delicate desires,
    All prompting me how fair young Hero is,
    Saying, I liked her ere I went to wars.
D. PEDRO.   Thou wilt be like a lover presently,
    And tire the hearer with a book of words.
    If thou dost love fair Hero, cherish it;
    And I will break[12] with her and with her father,
    And thou shalt have her. Was't not to this end
    That thou began'st to twist so fine a story?
CLAUD.   How sweetly you do minister to love,
    That know love's grief by his complexion!
    But lest my liking might too sudden seem,
    I would have salved it with a longer treatise.
D. PEDRO.   What need the bridge much broader than the flood?
    The fairest grant is the necessity.
    Look, what will serve is fit: 'tis once, thou lovest,
    And I will fit thee with the remedy.
    I know we shall have revelling to-night:
    I will assume thy part in some disguise,
    And tell fair Hero I am Claudio;
    And in her bosom I'll unclasp my heart,
    And take her hearing prisoner with the force
    And strong encounter of my amorous tale:
    Then after to her father will I break;
    And the conclusion is, she shall be thine.
    In practice let us put it presently.   [*Exeunt.*]

---

12. *break*] broach (the subject).

SCENE II. A *room in* LEONATO'S *house*.

Enter LEONATO *and* ANTONIO, *meeting*.

LEON.   How now, brother! Where is my cousin, your son? hath he
    provided this music?

ANT.   He is very busy about it. But, brother, I can tell you strange news,
    that you yet dreamt not of.

LEON.   Are they good?

ANT.   As the event stamps them: but they have a good cover; they show
    well outward. The prince and Count Claudio, walking in a thick-
    pleached[1] alley in mine orchard, were thus much overheard by a
    man of mine: the prince discovered[2] to Claudio that he loved my
    niece your daughter, and meant to acknowledge it this night in a
    dance; and if he found her accordant, he meant to take the present
    time by the top, and instantly break with you of it.

LEON.   Hath the fellow any wit that told you this?

ANT.   A good sharp fellow: I will send for him; and question him
    yourself.

LEON.   No, no; we will hold it as a dream till it appear itself: but I will
    acquaint my daughter withal, that she may be the better prepared
    for an answer, if peradventure this be true. Go you and tell her of it.
    [*Enter* Attendants.] Cousins, you know what you have to do. O, I
    cry you mercy, friend; go you with me, and I will use your skill.
    Good cousin, have a care this busy time.   [*Exeunt.*]

---

1. *thick-pleached*] with boughs thickly plaited or intertwined.
2. *discovered*] revealed.

SCENE III. *The same*.

Enter DON JOHN *and* CONRADE.

CON. What the good-year, my lord! why are you thus out of measure
sad?

D. JOHN. There is no measure in the occasion that breeds; therefore
the sadness is without limit.

CON. You should hear reason.

D. JOHN. And when I have heard it, what blessing brings it?

CON. If not a present remedy, at least a patient sufferance.

D. JOHN. I wonder that thou, being (as thou sayest thou art) born under
Saturn,[1] goest about to apply a moral medicine to a mortifying
mischief. I cannot hide what I am: I must be sad when I have cause,
and smile at no man's jests; eat when I have stomach, and wait for no
man's leisure; sleep when I am drowsy, and tend on no man's
business; laugh when I am merry, and claw no man in his humour.

CON. Yea, but you must not make the full show of this till you may do
it without controlment. You have of late stood out against your
brother, and he hath ta'en you newly into his grace; where it is
impossible you should take true root but by the fair weather that
you make yourself: it is needful that you frame the season for your
own harvest.

D. JOHN. I had rather be a canker in a hedge than a rose in his grace;
and it better fits my blood to be disdained of all than to fashion a
carriage to rob love from any: in this, though I cannot be said to be
a flattering honest man, it must not be denied but I am a plain-
dealing villain. I am trusted with a muzzle, and enfranchised with a
clog;[2] therefore I have decreed not to sing in my cage. If I had my

---

1. *born under Saturn*] of Saturnine or melancholy temperament.
2. *enfranchised with a clog*] set at liberty, but with a "clog" (anything hung upon an animal
to hinder motion).

mouth, I would bite; if I had my liberty, I would do my liking: in the meantime let me be that I am, and seek not to alter me.

CON. Can you make no use of your discontent?

D. JOHN. I make all use of it, for I use it only.
  Who comes here?

Enter BORACHIO.

What news, Borachio?

BORA. I came yonder from a great supper: the prince your brother is royally entertained by Leonato; and I can give you intelligence of an intended marriage.

D. JOHN. Will it serve for any model to build mischief on? What is he for a fool that betroths himself to unquietness?

BORA. Marry, it is your brother's right hand.

D. JOHN. Who? the most exquisite Claudio?

BORA. Even he.

D. JOHN. A proper squire! And who, and who? which way looks he?

BORA. Marry, on Hero, the daughter and heir of Leonato.

D. JOHN. A very forward March-chick! How came you to this?

BORA. Being entertained for a perfumer,[3] as I was smoking a musty room, comes me the prince and Claudio, hand in hand, in sad conference: I whipt me behind the arras; and there heard it agreed upon, that the prince should woo Hero for himself, and having obtained her, give her to Count Claudio.

D. JOHN. Come, come, let us thither: this may prove food to my displeasure. That young start-up hath all the glory of my overthrow: if I can cross him any way, I bless myself every way. You are both sure, and will assist me?

CON. To the death, my lord.

D. JOHN. Let us to the great supper: their cheer is the greater that I am subdued. Would the cook were of my mind! Shall we go prove what's to be done?

BORA. We'll wait upon your lordship.   [*Exeunt.*]

---

3. *entertained . . . perfumer*] Borachio is mistaken for someone who perfumes rooms by smoking aromatic herbs in a censer.

ACT II.

SCENE I. A *hall in* LEONATO'S *house*.

Enter LEONATO, ANTONIO, HERO, BEATRICE, *and others*.

LEON. Was not Count John here at supper?

ANT. I saw him not.

BEAT. How tartly that gentleman looks! I never can see him but I am heart-burned an hour after.

HERO. He is of a very melancholy disposition.

BEAT. He were an excellent man that were made just in the midway between him and Benedick: the one is too like an image and says nothing, and the other too like my lady's eldest son, evermore tattling.

LEON. Then half Signior Benedick's tongue in Count John's mouth, and half Count John's melancholy in Signior Benedick's face,—

BEAT. With a good leg and a good foot, uncle, and money enough in his purse, such a man would win any woman in the world, if a' could get her good-will.

LEON. By my troth, niece, thou wilt never get thee a husband, if thou be so shrewd[1] of thy tongue.

ANT. In faith, she's too curst.

BEAT. Too curst is more than curst: I shall lessen God's sending that way; for it is said, 'God sends a curst cow short horns;' but to a cow too curst he sends none.

LEON. So, by being too curst, God will send you no horns.

BEAT. Just, if he send me no husband; for the which blessing I am at

---

1. *shrewd*] vicious, bad-tempered.

him upon my knees every morning and evening. Lord, I could not endure a husband with a beard on his face: I had rather lie in the woollen.[2]

LEON.   You may light on a husband that hath no beard.

BEAT.   What should I do with him? dress him in my apparel, and make him my waiting-gentlewoman? He that hath a beard is more than a youth; and he that hath no beard is less than a man: and he that is more than a youth is not for me; and he that is less than a man, I am not for him: therefore I will even take sixpence in earnest of the bear-ward, and lead his apes into hell.

LEON.   Well, then, go you into hell?

BEAT.   No, but to the gate; and there will the devil meet me, like an old cuckold, with horns on his head, and say 'Get you to heaven, Beatrice, get you to heaven; here's no place for you maids:' so deliver I up my apes, and away to Saint Peter for the heavens; he shows me where the bachelors sit, and there live we as merry as the day is long.

ANT.   [*To Hero*] Well, niece, I trust you will be ruled by your father.

BEAT.   Yes, faith; it is my cousin's duty to make courtesy, and say, 'Father, as it please you.' But yet for all that, cousin, let him be a handsome fellow, or else make another courtesy, and say, 'Father, as it please me.'

LEON.   Well, niece, I hope to see you one day fitted with a husband.

BEAT.   Not till God make men of some other metal than earth. Would it not grieve a woman to be overmastered with a piece of valiant dust? to make an account of her life to a clod of wayward marl? No, uncle, I'll none: Adam's sons are my brethren; and, truly, I hold it a sin to match in my kindred.

LEON.   Daughter, remember what I told you: if the prince do solicit you in that kind, you know your answer.

BEAT.   The fault will be in the music, cousin, if you be not wooed in good time: if the prince be too important, tell him there is measure in every thing, and so dance out the answer. For, hear me, Hero: wooing, wedding, and repenting, is as a Scotch jig, a measure, and

2. *woollen*] shroud.

a cinque pace:[3] the first suit is hot and hasty, like a Scotch jig, and full as fantastical; the wedding, mannerly-modest, as a measure, full of state and ancientry; and then comes repentance, and, with his bad legs, falls into the cinque pace faster and faster, till he sink into his grave.

LEON.   Cousin, you apprehend passing shrewdly.

BEAT.   I have a good eye, uncle; I can see a church by daylight.

LEON.   The revellers are entering, brother: make good room.

                                    [*All put on their masks.*]

Enter DON PEDRO, CLAUDIO, BENEDICK, BALTHASAR, DON JOHN, BORACHIO, MARGARET, URSULA, *and others, masked.*

D. PEDRO.   Lady, will you walk about with your friend?

HERO.   So you walk softly, and look sweetly, and say nothing, I am yours for the walk; and especially when I walk away.

D. PEDRO.   With me in your company?

HERO.   I may say so, when I please.

D. PEDRO.   And when please you to say so?

HERO.   When I like your favour; for God defend the lute should be like the case!

D. PEDRO.   My visor is Philemon's roof; within the house is Jove.

HERO.   Why, then, your visor should be thatched.[4]

D. PEDRO.   Speak low, if you speak love.   [*Drawing her aside.*]

BALTH.   Well, I would you did like me.

MARG.   So would not I, for your own sake; for I have many ill qualities.

BALTH.   Which is one?

MARG.   I say my prayers aloud.

BALTH.   I love you the better: the hearers may cry, Amen.

MARG.   God match me with a good dancer!

BALTH.   Amen.

MARG.   And God keep him out of my sight when the dance is done! Answer, clerk.

---

3. *cinque pace*] the French dance called "cinq pas" or "galliard," of which each complete movement consisted of five steps; the pace quickened as the dance continued. The word is often written "sink-a-pace."

4. *Philemon's roof . . . thatched*] In Ovid's *Metamorphoses* (VIII, 630), two peasants, Philemon and Baucis, unknowingly entertained Jove and Mercury in their rustic thatch-roofed cottage.

BALTH.   No more words: the clerk is answered.

URS.   I know you well enough; you are Signior Antonio.

ANT.   At a word, I am not.

URS.   I know you by the waggling of your head.

ANT.   To tell you true, I counterfeit him.

URS.   You could never do him so ill-well, unless you were the very man. Here's his dry hand up and down: you are he, you are he.

ANT.   At a word, I am not.

URS.   Come, come, do you think I do not know you by your excellent wit? can virtue hide itself? Go to, mum, you are he: graces will appear, and there's an end.

BEAT.   Will you not tell me who told you so?

BENE.   No, you shall pardon me.

BEAT.   Nor will you not tell me who you are?

BENE.   Not now.

BEAT.   That I was disdainful, and that I had my good wit out of the 'Hundred Merry Tales':[5]—well, this was Signior Benedick that said so.

BENE.   What's he?

BEAT.   I am sure you know him well enough.

BENE.   Not I, believe me.

BEAT.   Did he never make you laugh?

BENE.   I pray you, what is he?

BEAT.   Why, he is the prince's jester: a very dull fool; only his gift is in devising impossible slanders: none but libertines delight in him; and the commendation is not in his wit, but in his villany; for he both pleases men and angers them, and then they laugh at him and beat him. I am sure he is in the fleet: I would he had boarded me.

BENE.   When I know the gentleman, I'll tell him what you say.

BEAT.   Do, do: he'll but break a comparison or two on me; which, peradventure not marked or not laughed at, strikes him into melancholy; and then there's a partridge wing saved, for the fool will eat no supper that night. [*Music.*] We must follow the leaders.

BENE.   In every good thing.

BEAT.   Nay, if they lead to any ill, I will leave them at the next turning.

---

5. *'Hundred Merry Tales'*] the title of a popular joke book, first published in 1526 and frequently reissued.

[*Dance. Then exeunt all except* DON JOHN, BORACHIO, *and* CLAUDIO.]

D. JOHN.   Sure my brother is amorous on Hero, and hath withdrawn
     her father to break with him about it. The ladies follow her, and but
     one visor remains.

BORA.   And that is Claudio: I know him by his bearing.

D. JOHN.   Are not you Signior Benedick?

CLAUD.   You know me well; I am he.

D. JOHN.   Signior, you are very near my brother in his love: he
     is enamoured on Hero; I pray you, dissuade him from her: she is
     no equal for his birth: you may do the part of an honest man
     in it.

CLAUD.   How know you he loves her?

D. JOHN.   I heard him swear his affection.

BORA.   So did I too; and he swore he would marry her to-night.

D. JOHN.   Come, let us to the banquet.

                              [*Exeunt* DON JOHN *and* BORACHIO.]

CLAUD.   Thus answer I in name of Benedick,
     But hear these ill news with the ears of Claudio.
     'Tis certain so; the prince wooes for himself.
     Friendship is constant in all other things
     Save in the office and affairs of love:
     Therefore all hearts in love use their own tongues;
     Let every eye negotiate for itself,
     And trust no agent; for beauty is a witch,
     Against whose charms faith melteth into blood.
     This is an accident of hourly proof,
     Which I mistrusted not. Farewell, therefore, Hero!

Re-enter BENEDICK.

BENE.   Count Claudio?

CLAUD.   Yea, the same.

BENE.   Come, will you go with me?

CLAUD.   Whither?

BENE.   Even to the next willow, about your own business, county.
     What fashion will you wear the garland of? about your neck, like an
     usurer's chain? or under your arm, like a lieutenant's scarf? You
     must wear it one way, for the prince hath got your Hero.

CLAUD.   I wish him joy of her.

BENE.   Why, that's spoken like an honest drovier;[6] so they sell bullocks. But did you think the prince would have served you thus?

CLAUD.   I pray you, leave me.

BENE.   Ho! now you strike like the blind man; 'twas the boy that stole your meat, and you'll beat the post.

CLAUD.   If it will not be, I'll leave you.   [*Exit.*]

BENE.   Alas, poor hurt fowl! now will he creep into sedges. But, that my Lady Beatrice should know me, and not know me! The prince's fool! Ha? It may be I go under that title because I am merry. Yea, but so I am apt to do myself wrong; I am not so reputed: it is the base, though bitter, disposition of Beatrice that puts the world into her person, and so gives me out. Well, I'll be revenged as I may.

Re-enter DON PEDRO.

D. PEDRO.   Now, signior, where's the count? did you see him?

BENE.   Troth, my lord, I have played the part of Lady Fame. I found him here as melancholy as a lodge in a warren:[7] I told him, and I think I told him true, that your grace had got the good will of this young lady; and I offered him my company to a willow-tree, either to make him a garland, as being forsaken, or to bind him up a rod, as being worthy to be whipped.

D. PEDRO.   To be whipped! What's his fault?

BENE.   The flat transgression of a school-boy, who, being overjoyed with finding a birds' nest, shows it his companion, and he steals it.

D. PEDRO.   Wilt thou make a trust a transgression? The transgression is in the stealer.

BENE.   Yet it had not been amiss the rod had been made, and the garland too; for the garland he might have worn himself, and the rod he might have bestowed on you, who, as I take it, have stolen his birds' nest.

D. PEDRO.   I will but teach them to sing, and restore them to the owner.

BENE.   If their singing answer your saying, by my faith, you say honestly.

---

6. *drovier*] cattle dealer.
7. *a lodge in a warren*] a keeper's hut, necessarily isolated in a game preserve.

D. PEDRO.   The Lady Beatrice hath a quarrel to you: the gentleman
that danced with her told her she is much wronged by you.

BENE.   O, she misused me past the endurance of a block! an oak but
with one green leaf on it would have answered her; my very visor
began to assume life and scold with her. She told me, not thinking I
had been myself, that I was the prince's jester, that I was duller than
a great thaw; huddling jest upon jest, with such impossible convey-
ance, upon me, that I stood like a man at a mark, with a whole army
shooting at me. She speaks poniards, and every word stabs: if her
breath were as terrible as her terminations,[8] there were no living
near her; she would infect to the north star. I would not marry her,
though she were endowed with all that Adam had left him before
he transgressed: she would have made Hercules have turned spit,
yea, and have cleft his club to make the fire too. Come, talk not of
her: you shall find her the infernal Ate[9] in good apparel. I would to
God some scholar would conjure[10] her; for certainly, while she is
here, a man may live as quiet in hell as in a sanctuary; and people
sin upon purpose, because they would go thither; so, indeed, all
disquiet, horror, and perturbation follows her.

D. PEDRO.   Look, here she comes.

Re-enter CLAUDIO, BEATRICE, HERO, *and* LEONATO.

BENE.   Will your grace command me any service to the world's end? I
will go on the slightest errand now to the Antipodes that you can
devise to send me on; I will fetch you a toothpicker now from the
furthest inch of Asia; bring you the length of Prester John's foot;
fetch you a hair off the great Cham's beard; do you any embassage
to the Pigmies;[11] rather than hold three words' conference with this
harpy. You have no employment for me?

D. PEDRO.   None, but to desire your good company.

---

8. *terminations*] terms, epithets.
9. *Ate*] the spirit of discord in Homeric mythology.
10. *conjure*] exorcise; exorcisms were performed in Latin, so the exorcist would have to be
    a scholar.
11. *Prester John's foot . . . Cham's beard . . . Pigmies*] according to romances, Prester John
    was an Asian king of vast wealth; Cham was the supreme ruler of the Mongols; the
    Pigmies were a tribe in the northern mountains of India.

BENE.   O God, sir, here's a dish I love not: I cannot endure my Lady
   Tongue.   [*Exit.*]
D. PEDRO.   Come, lady, come; you have lost the heart of Signior
   Benedick.
BEAT.   Indeed, my lord, he lent it me awhile; and I gave him use for it,
   a double heart for his single one: marry, once before he won it of
   me with false dice, therefore your Grace may well say I have lost it.
D. PEDRO.   You have put him down, lady, you have put him down.
BEAT.   So I would not he should do me, my lord, lest I should prove the
   mother of fools. I have brought Count Claudio, whom you sent me
   to seek.
D. PEDRO.   Why, how now, count! wherefore are you sad?
CLAUD.   Not sad, my lord.
D. PEDRO.   How then? sick?
CLAUD.   Neither, my lord.
BEAT.   The count is neither sad, nor sick, nor merry, nor well; but civil
   count, civil as an orange, and something of that jealous complexion.
D. PEDRO.   I' faith, lady, I think your blazon to be true; though, I'll be
   sworn, if he be so, his conceit is false. Here, Claudio, I have wooed in
   thy name, and fair Hero is won: I have broke with her father, and his
   good will obtained: name the day of marriage, and God give thee joy!
LEON.   Count, take of me my daughter, and with her my fortunes: his
   Grace hath made the match, and all grace say Amen to it.
BEAT.   Speak, count, 'tis your cue.
CLAUD.   Silence is the perfectest herald of joy: I were but little happy,
   if I could say how much. Lady, as you are mine, I am yours: I give
   away myself for you, and dote upon the exchange.
BEAT.   Speak, cousin; or, if you cannot, stop his mouth with a kiss, and
   let not him speak neither.
D. PEDRO.   In faith, lady, you have a merry heart.
BEAT.   Yea, my lord; I thank it, poor fool, it keeps on the windy side of
   care. My cousin tells him in his ear that he is in her heart.
CLAUD.   And so she doth, cousin.
BEAT.   Good Lord, for alliance! Thus goes every one to the world but I,
   and I am sun-burnt;[12] I may sit in a corner, and cry heigh-ho for a
   husband!

12. *sun-burnt*] neglected, exposed to the weather, homely, plain.

D. PEDRO.   Lady Beatrice, I will get you one.

BEAT.   I would rather have one of your father's getting. Hath your Grace ne'er a brother like you? Your father got excellent husbands, if a maid could come by them.

D. PEDRO.   Will you have me, lady?

BEAT.   No, my lord, unless I might have another for working-days: your Grace is too costly to wear every day. But, I beseech your Grace, pardon me: I was born to speak all mirth and no matter.

D. PEDRO.   Your silence most offends me, and to be merry best becomes you; for, out of question, you were born in a merry hour.

BEAT.   No, sure, my lord, my mother cried; but then there was a star danced, and under that was I born. Cousins, God give you joy!

LEON.   Niece, will you look to those things I told you of?

BEAT.   I cry you mercy, uncle. By your Grace's pardon.   [*Exit.*]

D. PEDRO.   By my troth, a pleasant-spirited lady.

LEON.   There's little of the melancholy element in her, my lord: she is never sad but when she sleeps; and not ever sad then; for I have heard my daughter say, she hath often dreamed of unhappiness, and waked herself with laughing.

D. PEDRO.   She cannot endure to hear tell of a husband.

LEON.   O, by no means: she mocks all her wooers out of suit.

D. PEDRO.   She were an excellent wife for Benedick.

LEON.   O Lord, my lord, if they were but a week married, they would talk themselves mad.

D. PEDRO.   County Claudio, when mean you to go to church?

CLAUD.   To-morrow, my lord: time goes on crutches till love have all his rites.

LEON.   Not till Monday, my dear son, which is hence a just seven-night; and a time too brief, too, to have all things answer my mind.

D. PEDRO.   Come, you shake the head at so long a breathing: but, I warrant thee, Claudio, the time shall not go dully by us. I will, in the interim, undertake one of Hercules' labours; which is, to bring Signior Benedick and the Lady Beatrice into a mountain of affection the one with the other. I would fain have it a match; and I doubt not but to fashion it, if you three will but minister such assistance as I shall give you direction.

LEON.   My lord, I am for you, though it cost me ten nights' watchings.

CLAUD.   And I, my lord.

D. PEDRO.   And you too, gentle Hero?

HERO.   I will do any modest office, my lord, to help my cousin to a good husband.

D. PEDRO.   And Benedick is not the unhopefullest husband that I know. Thus far can I praise him; he is of a noble strain, of approved valour, and confirmed honesty. I will teach you how to humour your cousin, that she shall fall in love with Benedick; and I, with your two helps, will so practise on Benedick, that, in despite of his quick wit and his queasy stomach, he shall fall in love with Beatrice. If we can do this, Cupid is no longer an archer: his glory shall be ours, for we are the only love-gods. Go in with me, and I will tell you my drift.   [*Exeunt.*]

SCENE II. *The same.*

Enter DON JOHN *and* BORACHIO.

D. JOHN.   It is so; the Count Claudio shall marry the daughter of Leonato.

BORA.   Yea, my lord; but I can cross it.

D. JOHN.   Any bar, any cross, any impediment will be medicinable to me: I am sick in displeasure to him; and whatsoever comes athwart his affection ranges evenly with mine. How canst thou cross this marriage?

BORA.   Not honestly, my lord; but so covertly that no dishonesty shall appear in me.

D. JOHN.   Show me briefly how.

BORA.   I think I told your lordship, a year since, how much I am in the favour of Margaret, the waiting gentlewoman to Hero.

D. JOHN.   I remember.

BORA.   I can, at any unseasonable instant of the night, appoint her to look out at her lady's chamber window.

D. JOHN.   What life is in that, to be the death of this marriage?

BORA.   The poison of that lies in you to temper. Go you to the prince your brother; spare not to tell him that he hath wronged his honour in marrying the renowned Claudio—whose estimation do you mightily hold up—to a contaminated stale, such a one as Hero.

D. JOHN.   What proof shall I make of that?

BORA.   Proof enough to misuse the prince, to vex Claudio, to undo Hero, and kill Leonato. Look you for any other issue?

D. JOHN.   Only to despite them I will endeavour any thing.

BORA.   Go, then; find me a meet hour to draw Don Pedro and the Count Claudio alone: tell them that you know that Hero loves me; intend[1] a kind of zeal both to the prince and Claudio, as,—in love of your brother's honour, who hath made this match, and his friend's reputation, who is thus like to be cozened with the semblance of a maid,—that you have discovered thus. They will scarcely believe this without trial: offer them instances; which shall bear no less likelihood than to see me at her chamber-window; hear me call Margaret, Hero; hear Margaret term me Claudio; and bring them to see this the very night before the intended wedding,—for in the meantime I will so fashion the matter that Hero shall be absent,—and there shall appear such seeming truth of Hero's disloyalty, that jealousy shall be called assurance and all the preparation overthrown.

D. JOHN.   Grow this to what adverse issue it can, I will put it in practice. Be cunning in the working this, and thy fee is a thousand ducats.

BORA.   Be you constant in the accusation, and my cunning shall not shame me.

D. JOHN.   I will presently go learn their day of marriage.

[Exeunt.]

---

1. *intend*] pretend.

SCENE III. LEONATO'S *orchard*.

Enter BENEDICK.

BENE.   Boy!

Enter Boy.

BOY.   Signior?

BENE.   In my chamber-window lies a book: bring it hither to me in the orchard.

BOY.   I am here already, sir.

BENE.   I know that; but I would have thee hence, and here again. [*Exit* Boy.] I do much wonder that one man, seeing how much another man is a fool when he dedicates his behaviours to love, will, after he hath laughed at such shallow follies in others, become the argument of his own scorn by falling in love: and such a man is Claudio. I have known when there was no music with him but the drum and the fife; and now had he rather hear the tabor and the pipe: I have known when he would have walked ten mile a-foot to see a good armour; and now will he lie ten nights awake, carving the fashion of a new doublet. He was wont to speak plain and to the purpose, like an honest man and a soldier; and now is he turned orthography; his words are a very fantastical banquet,—just so many strange dishes. May I be so converted, and see with these eyes? I cannot tell; I think not: I will not be sworn but love may transform me to an oyster; but I'll take my oath on it, till he have made an oyster of me, he shall never make me such a fool. One woman is fair, yet I am well; another is wise, yet I am well; another virtuous, yet I am well: but till all graces be in one woman, one woman shall not come in my grace. Rich she shall be, that's certain; wise, or I'll none; virtuous, or I'll never cheapen her; fair, or I'll never look on her; mild, or come not near me; noble, or not I for an angel; of good discourse, an excellent musician, and her hair shall be of what colour it please God. Ha! the prince and Monsieur Love! I will hide me in the arbour.   [*Withdraws.*]

Enter DON PEDRO, CLAUDIO, *and* LEONATO.

D. PEDRO.   Come, shall we hear this music?
CLAUD.   Yea, my good lord. How still the evening is,
    As hush'd on purpose to grace harmony!
D. PEDRO.   See you where Benedick hath hid himself?
CLAUD.   O, very well, my lord: the music ended,
    We'll fit the kid-fox with a pennyworth.

Enter BALTHASAR *with Music.*

D. PEDRO.   Come, Balthasar, we'll hear that song again.
BALTH.   O, good my lord, tax not so bad a voice
    To slander music any more than once.
D. PEDRO.   It is the witness still of excellency
    To put a strange face on his own perfection.
    I pray thee, sing, and let me woo no more.
BALTH.   Because you talk of wooing, I will sing;
    Since many a wooer doth commence his suit
    To her he thinks not worthy, yet he wooes,
    Yet will he swear he loves.
D. PEDRO.   Nay, pray thee, come;
    Or, if thou wilt hold longer argument,
    Do it in notes.
BALTH.   Note this before my notes;
    There's not a note of mine that's worth the noting.
D. PEDRO.   Why, these are very crotchets[1] that he speaks;
    Note, notes, forsooth, and nothing.   [*Air.*]
BENE.   Now, divine air! now is his soul ravished! Is it not strange that
    sheeps' guts should hale souls out of men's bodies? Well, a horn for
    my money, when all's done.

BALTH.   The Song.

        Sigh no more, ladies, sigh no more,
          Men were deceivers ever,
        One foot in sea and one on shore,
          To one thing constant never:

---

1. *crotchets*] perverse conceits; also, characters in music.

Then sigh not so, but let them go,
And be you blithe and bonny,
Converting all your sounds of woe
Into Hey nonny, nonny.

Sing no more ditties, sing no moe,
Of dumps so dull and heavy;
The fraud of men was ever so,
Since summer first was leavy:[2]
Then sigh not so, &c.

D. PEDRO.   By my troth, a good song.

BALTH.   And an ill singer, my lord.

D. PEDRO.   Ha, no, no, faith; thou singest well enough for a shift.

BENE.   An[3] he had been a dog that should have howled thus, they
would have hanged him: and I pray God his bad voice bode no
mischief. I had as lief have heard the night-raven, come what
plague could have come after it.

D. PEDRO.   Yea, marry, dost thou hear, Balthasar? I pray thee, get us
some excellent music; for to-morrow night we would have it at the
Lady Hero's chamber-window.

BALTH.   The best I can, my lord.

D. PEDRO.   Do so: farewell. [*Exit* BALTHASAR.] Come hither, Leonato.
What was it you told me of to-day, that your niece Beatrice was in
love with Signior Benedick?

CLAUD.   O, ay: stalk on, stalk on; the fowl sits. I did never think that
lady would have loved any man.

LEON.   No, nor I neither; but most wonderful that she should so dote
on Signior Benedick, whom she hath in all outward behaviours
seemed ever to abhor.

BENE.   Is't possible? Sits the wind in that corner?

LEON.   By my troth, my lord, I cannot tell what to think of it, but that
she loves him with an enraged affection; it is past the infinite of
thought.

D. PEDRO.   May be she doth but counterfeit.

CLAUD.   Faith, like enough.

---

2. *leavy*] full of leaves.
3. *An*] if.

LEON.   O God, counterfeit! There was never counterfeit of passion came so near the life of passion as she discovers it.

D. PEDRO.   Why, what effects of passion shows she?

CLAUD.   Bait the hook well; this fish will bite.

LEON.   What effects, my lord? She will sit you, you heard my daughter tell you how.

CLAUD.   She did, indeed.

D. PEDRO.   How, how, I pray you? You amaze me: I would have thought her spirit had been invincible against all assaults of affection.

LEON.   I would have sworn it had, my lord; especially against Benedick.

BENE.   I should think this a gull,[4] but that the white-bearded fellow speaks it: knavery cannot, sure, hide himself in such reverence.

CLAUD.   He hath ta'en the infection: hold it up.

D. PEDRO.   Hath she made her affection known to Benedick?

LEON.   No; and swears she never will: that's her torment.

CLAUD.   'Tis true, indeed; so your daughter says: 'Shall I,' says she, 'that have so oft encountered him with scorn, write to him that I love him?'

LEON.   This says she now when she is beginning to write to him; for she'll be up twenty times a night; and there will she sit in her smock till she have writ a sheet of paper: my daughter tells us all.

CLAUD.   Now you talk of a sheet of paper, I remember a pretty jest your daughter told us of.

LEON.   O, when she had writ it, and was reading it over, she found Benedick and Beatrice between the sheet?

CLAUD.   That.

LEON.   O, she tore the letter into a thousand halfpence; railed at herself, that she should be so immodest to write to one that she knew would flout her; 'I measure him,' says she, 'by my own spirit; for I should flout him, if he writ to me; yea, though I love him, I should.'

CLAUD.   Then down upon her knees she falls, weeps, sobs, beats her heart, tears her hair, prays, curses; 'O sweet Benedick! God give me patience!'

---

4. *gull*] trick.

LEON.   She doth indeed; my daughter says so: and the ecstasy hath so much overborne her, that my daughter is sometime afeard she will do a desperate outrage to herself: it is very true.

D. PEDRO.   It were good that Benedick knew of it by some other, if she will not discover it.

CLAUD.   To what end? He would make but a sport of it, and torment the poor lady worse.

D. PEDRO.   An he should, it were an alms to hang him. She's an excellent sweet lady; and, out of all suspicion, she is virtuous.

CLAUD.   And she is exceeding wise.

D. PEDRO.   In every thing but in loving Benedick.

LEON.   O, my lord, wisdom and blood combating in so tender a body, we have ten proofs to one that blood hath the victory. I am sorry for her, as I have just cause, being her uncle and her guardian.

D. PEDRO.   I would she had bestowed this dotage on me: I would have daffed[5] all other respects, and made her half myself. I pray you, tell Benedick of it, and hear what a' will say.

LEON.   Were it good, think you?

CLAUD.   Hero thinks surely she will die; for she says she will die, if he love her not; and she will die, ere she make her love known; and she will die, if he woo her, rather than she will bate one breath of her accustomed crossness.

D. PEDRO.   She doth well: if she should make tender[6] of her love, 'tis very possible he'll scorn it; for the man, as you know all, hath a contemptible spirit.

CLAUD.   He is a very proper man.

D. PEDRO.   He hath indeed a good outward happiness.

CLAUD.   Before God! and in my mind, very wise.

D. PEDRO.   He doth indeed show some sparks that are like wit.

CLAUD.   And I take him to be valiant.

D. PEDRO.   As Hector, I assure you: and in the managing of quarrels you may say he is wise; for either he avoids them with great discretion, or undertakes them with a most Christian-like fear.

LEON.   If he do fear God, a' must necessarily keep peace: if he break the peace, he ought to enter into a quarrel with fear and trembling.

---

5. *daffed*] doffed, put aside.
6. *tender*] an offer for acceptance.

D. PEDRO.   And so will he do; for the man doth fear God, howsoever it seems not in him by some large jests he will make. Well, I am sorry for your niece. Shall we go seek Benedick, and tell him of her love?

CLAUD.   Never tell him, my lord: let her wear it out with good counsel.

LEON.   Nay, that's impossible: she may wear her heart out first.

D. PEDRO.   Well, we will hear further of it by your daughter: let it cool the while. I love Benedick well; and I could wish he would modestly examine himself, to see how much he is unworthy so good a lady.

LEON.   My lord, will you walk? dinner is ready.

CLAUD.   If he do not dote on her upon this, I will never trust my expectation.

D. PEDRO.   Let there be the same net spread for her; and that must your daughter and her gentlewomen carry. The sport will be, when they hold one an opinion of another's dotage, and no such matter: that's the scene that I would see, which will be merely a dumb-show. Let us send her to call him in to dinner.

[*Exeunt* DON PEDRO, CLAUDIO, *and* LEONATO.]

BENE.   [*Coming forward*] This can be no trick: the conference was sadly borne. They have the truth of this from Hero. They seem to pity the lady: it seems her affections have their full bent. Love me! why, it must be requited. I hear how I am censured: they say I will bear myself proudly, if I perceive the love come from her; they say too that she will rather die than give any sign of affection. I did never think to marry: I must not seem proud: happy are they that hear their detractions, and can put them to mending. They say the lady is fair, — 'tis a truth, I can bear them witness; and virtuous, — 'tis so, I cannot reprove it; and wise, but for loving me, — by my troth, it is no addition to her wit, nor no great argument of her folly, for I will be horribly in love with her. I may chance have some odd quirks and remnants of wit broken on me, because I have railed so long against marriage: but doth not the appetite alter? a man loves the meat in his youth that he cannot endure in his age. Shall quips and sentences and these paper bullets[7] of the brain awe a man from the career of his humour? No, the world must be peopled. When I said I would die a bachelor, I did not think I should live till I were married. Here comes Beatrice. By this day! she's a fair lady: I do spy some marks of love in her.

---

7. *paper bullets*] epigrams from books.

Enter BEATRICE.

BEAT.   Against my will I am sent to bid you come in to dinner.

BENE.   Fair Beatrice, I thank you for your pains.

BEAT.   I took no more pains for those thanks than you take pains to thank me: if it had been painful, I would not have come.

BENE.   You take pleasure, then, in the message?

BEAT.   Yea, just so much as you may take upon a knife's point, and choke a daw withal. You have no stomach, signior: fare you well.

[Exit.]

BENE.   Ha! 'Against my will I am sent to bid you come in to dinner;' there's a double meaning in that. 'I took no more pains for those thanks than you took pains to thank me;' that's as much as to say, Any pains that I take for you is as easy as thanks. If I do not take pity of her, I am a villain; if I do not love her, I am a Jew. I will go get her picture.

[Exit.]

ACT III.

SCENE I. LEONATO'S *orchard.*

Enter HERO, MARGARET, *and* URSULA.

HERO.   Good Margaret, run thee to the parlour;
There shalt thou find my cousin Beatrice
Proposing with the prince and Claudio:
Whisper her ear, and tell her, I and Ursula
Walk in the orchard, and our whole discourse
Is all of her; say that thou overheard'st us;
And bid her steal into the pleached bower,
Where honeysuckles, ripen'd by the sun,
Forbid the sun to enter; like favourites,
Made proud by princes, that advance their pride
Against that power that bred it: there will she hide her,
To listen our propose. This is thy office;
Bear thee well in it, and leave us alone.
MARG.   I'll make her come, I warrant you, presently.   [*Exit.*]
HERO.   Now, Ursula, when Beatrice doth come,
As we do trace this alley up and down,
Our talk must only be of Benedick.
When I do name him, let it be thy part
To praise him more than ever man did merit:
My talk to thee must be, how Benedick
Is sick in love with Beatrice. Of this matter
Is little Cupid's crafty arrow made,
That only wounds by hearsay.

31

Enter BEATRICE, *behind.*

                        Now begin;
    For look where Beatrice, like a lapwing, runs
    Close by the ground, to hear our conference.
URS.   The pleasant'st angling is to see the fish
    Cut with her golden oars the silver stream,
    And greedily devour the treacherous bait:
    So angle we for Beatrice; who even now
    Is couched in the woodbine coverture.
    Fear you not my part of the dialogue.
HERO.   Then go we near her, that her ear lose nothing
    Of the false sweet bait that we lay for it.

                        [*Approaching the bower.*]

    No, truly, Ursula, she is too disdainful;
    I know her spirits are as coy and wild
    As haggerds[1] of the rock.
URS.   But are you sure
    That Benedick loves Beatrice so entirely?
HERO.   So says the prince and my new-trothed lord.
URS.   And did they bid you tell her of it, madam?
HERO.   They did entreat me to acquaint her of it;
    But I persuaded them, if they loved Benedick,
    To wish him wrestle with affection,
    And never to let Beatrice know of it.
URS.   Why did you so? Doth not the gentleman
    Deserve as full as fortunate a bed
    As ever Beatrice shall couch upon?
HERO.   O god of love! I know he doth deserve
    As much as may be yielded to a man:
    But Nature never framed a woman's heart
    Of prouder stuff than that of Beatrice;
    Disdain and scorn ride sparkling in her eyes,
    Misprising what they look on; and her wit
    Values itself so highly, that to her
    All matter else seems weak: she cannot love,

---

1. *haggerds*] haggards; wild, untrained hawks.

     Nor take no shape nor project of affection,
     She is so self-endeared.

URS.   Sure, I think so;
     And therefore certainly it were not good
     She knew his love, lest she make sport at it.

HERO.   Why, you speak truth. I never yet saw man,
     How wise, how noble, young, how rarely featured,
     But she would spell him backward: if fair-faced,
     She would swear the gentleman should be her sister;
     If black, why, Nature, drawing of an antique,
     Made a foul blot; if tall, a lance ill-headed;
     If low, an agate very vilely cut;
     If speaking, why, a vane blown with all winds;
     If silent, why, a block moved with none.
     So turns she every man the wrong side out;
     And never gives to truth and virtue that
     Which simpleness and merit purchaseth.

URS.   Sure, sure, such carping is not commendable.

HERO.   No, not to be so odd, and from all fashions,
     As Beatrice is, cannot be commendable:
     But who dare tell her so? If I should speak,
     She would mock me into air; O, she would laugh me
     Out of myself, press me to death with wit!
     Therefore let Benedick, like cover'd fire,
     Consume away in sighs, waste inwardly:
     It were a better death than die with mocks,
     Which is as bad as die with tickling.

URS.   Yet tell her of it: hear what she will say.

HERO.   No; rather I will go to Benedick,
     And counsel him to fight against his passion.
     And, truly, I'll devise some honest slanders
     To stain my cousin with: one doth not know
     How much an ill word may empoison liking.

URS.   O, do not do your cousin such a wrong!
     She cannot be so much without true judgement,—
     Having so swift and excellent a wit
     As she is prized to have,—as to refuse
     So rare a gentleman as Signior Benedick.

HERO.   He is the only man of Italy,

Always excepted my dear Claudio.

URS.   I pray you, be not angry with me, madam,
Speaking my fancy: Signior Benedick,
For shape, for bearing, argument and valour,
Goes foremost in report through Italy.

HERO.   Indeed, he hath an excellent good name.

URS.   His excellence did earn it, ere he had it.
When are you married, madam?

HERO.   Why, every day, to-morrow. Come, go in:
I'll show thee some attires; and have thy counsel
Which is the best to furnish me to-morrow.

URS.   She's limed,[2] I warrant you: we have caught her, madam.

HERO.   If it prove so, then loving goes by haps:
Some Cupid kills with arrows, some with traps.

[*Exeunt* HERO *and* URSULA.]

BEAT.   [*Coming forward*] What fire is in mine ears? Can this be true?
Stand I condemn'd for pride and scorn so much?
Contempt, farewell! and maiden pride, adieu!
No glory lives behind the back of such.
And, Benedick, love on; I will requite thee,
Taming my wild heart to thy loving hand:
If thou dost love, my kindness shall incite thee
To bind our loves up in a holy band;
For others say thou dost deserve, and I
Believe it better than reportingly.   [*Exit.*]

SCENE II. *A room in* LEONATO'S *house.*

Enter DON PEDRO, CLAUDIO, BENEDICK, *and* LEONATO.

D. PEDRO.   I do but stay till your marriage be consummate, and then
go I toward Arragon.

CLAUD.   I'll bring you thither, my lord, if you'll vouchsafe me.

---

2. *limed*] trapped, ensnared as a bird with birdlime, a glutinous substance used to catch
birds.

D. PEDRO.   Nay, that would be as great a soil in the new gloss of your marriage, as to show a child his new coat and forbid him to wear it. I will only be bold with Benedick for his company; for, from the crown of his head to the sole of his foot, he is all mirth: he hath twice or thrice cut Cupid's bow-string, and the little hangman dare not shoot at him; he hath a heart as sound as a bell, and his tongue is the clapper, for what his heart thinks his tongue speaks.

BENE.   Gallants, I am not as I have been.

LEON.   So say I: methinks you are sadder.

CLAUD.   I hope he be in love.

D. PEDRO.   Hang him, truant! there's no true drop of blood in him, to be truly touched with love; if he be sad, he wants money.

BENE.   I have the toothache.

D. PEDRO.   Draw it.

BENE.   Hang it!

CLAUD.   You must hang it first, and draw it afterwards.[1]

D. PEDRO.   What! sigh for the toothache?

LEON.   Where is but a humour or a worm.

BENE.   Well, every one can master a grief but he that has it.

CLAUD.   Yet say I, he is in love.

D. PEDRO.   There is no appearance of fancy in him, unless it be a fancy that he hath to strange disguises; as, to be a Dutchman to-day, a Frenchman to-morrow; or in the shape of two countries at once, as, a German from the waist downward, all slops,[2] and a Spaniard from the hip upward, no doublet. Unless he have a fancy to this foolery, as it appears he hath, he is no fool for fancy, as you would have it appear he is.

CLAUD.   If he be not in love with some woman, there is no believing old signs: a' brushes his hat o' mornings; what should that bode?

D. PEDRO.   Hath any man seen him at the barber's?

CLAUD.   No, but the barber's man hath been seen with him; and the old ornament of his cheek hath already stuffed tennis-balls.

LEON.   Indeed, he looks younger than he did, by the loss of a beard.

---

1. *You must hang . . . afterwards*] an allusion to the punishment of "drawing," i.e., disembowelment, which followed hanging and preceded "quartering" (dividing the body into four parts) in convictions of treason.
2. *slops*] loose, ill-fitting trousers.

D. PEDRO. Nay, a' rubs himself with civet:[3] can you smell him out by that?

CLAUD. That's as much as to say, the sweet youth's in love.

D. PEDRO. The greatest note of it is his melancholy.

CLAUD. And when was he wont to wash his face?

D. PEDRO. Yea, or to paint himself? for the which, I hear what they say of him.

CLAUD. Nay, but his jesting spirit; which is now crept into a lute-string, and now governed by stops.[4]

D. PEDRO. Indeed, that tells a heavy tale for him: conclude, conclude he is in love.

CLAUD. Nay, but I know who loves him.

D. PEDRO. That would I know too: I warrant, one that knows him not.

CLAUD. Yes, and his ill conditions; and, in despite of all, dies for him.

D. PEDRO. She shall be buried with her face upwards.

BENE. Yet is this no charm for the toothache. Old signior, walk aside with me: I have studied eight or nine wise words to speak to you, which these hobby-horses must not hear.

> [*Exeunt* BENEDICK *and* LEONATO.]

D. PEDRO. For my life, to break with him about Beatrice.

CLAUD. 'Tis even so. Hero and Margaret have by this played their parts with Beatrice; and then the two bears will not bite one another when they meet.

Enter DON JOHN.

D. JOHN. My lord and brother, God save you!

D. PEDRO. Good den,[5] brother.

D. JOHN. If your leisure served, I would speak with you.

D. PEDRO. In private?

D. JOHN. If it please you: yet Count Claudio may hear; for what I would speak of concerns him.

D. PEDRO. What's the matter?

D. JOHN. [*To* CLAUDIO] Means your lordship to be married to-morrow?

---

3. *civet*] a perfume from the civet-cat.
4. *stops*] marks on the lute's fingerboard that indicate where the fingers should be pressed to produce various notes.
5. *den*] abbreviation for evening.

D. PEDRO. You know he does.

D. JOHN. I know not that, when he knows what I know.

CLAUD. If there be any impediment, I pray you discover it.

D. JOHN. You may think I love you not: let that appear hereafter, and aim better at me by that I now will manifest. For my brother, I think he holds you well, and in dearness of heart hath holp to effect your ensuing marriage,—surely suit ill spent and labour ill bestowed.

D. PEDRO. Why, what's the matter?

D. JOHN. I came hither to tell you; and, circumstances shortened, for she has been too long a talking of, the lady is disloyal.

CLAUD. Who, Hero?

D. JOHN. Even she; Leonato's Hero, your Hero, every man's Hero.

CLAUD. Disloyal?

D. JOHN. The word is too good to paint out her wickedness; I could say she were worse: think you of a worse title, and I will fit her to it. Wonder not till further warrant: go but with me to-night, you shall see her chamber-window entered, even the night before her wedding-day: if you love her then, to-morrow wed her; but it would better fit your honour to change your mind.

CLAUD. May this be so?

D. PEDRO. I will not think it.

D. JOHN. If you dare not trust that you see, confess not that you know: if you will follow me, I will show you enough; and when you have seen more, and heard more, proceed accordingly.

CLAUD. If I see any thing to-night why I should not marry her to-morrow, in the congregation, where I should wed, there will I shame her.

D. PEDRO. And, as I wooed for thee to obtain her, I will join with thee to disgrace her.

D. JOHN. I will disparage her no farther till you are my witnesses: bear it coldly but till midnight, and let the issue show itself.

D. PEDRO. O day untowardly turned!

CLAUD. O mischief strangely thwarting!

D. JOHN. O plague right well prevented! so will you say when you have seen the sequel.   *[Exeunt.]*

Scene III. *A street*.

Enter Dogberry *and* Verges *with the* Watch.

Dog.   Are you good men and true?

Verg.   Yea, or else it were pity but they should suffer salvation, body
and soul.

Dog.   Nay, that were a punishment too good for them, if they should
have any allegiance in them, being chosen for the prince's watch.

Verg.   Well, give them their charge, neighbour Dogberry.

Dog.   First, who think you the most desartless man to be constable?

First Watch.   Hugh Otecake, sir, or George Seacole; for they can
write and read.

Dog.   Come hither, neighbour Seacole. God hath blessed you with a
good name: to be a well-favoured man is the gift of fortune; but to
write and read comes by nature.

Sec. Watch.   Both which, master constable,—

Dog.   You have: I knew it would be your answer. Well, for your favour,
sir, why, give God thanks, and make no boast of it; and for your
writing and reading, let that appear when there is no need of such
vanity. You are thought here to be the most senseless[1] and fit man
for the constable of the watch; therefore bear you the lantern. This
is your charge: you shall comprehend[2] all vagrom[3] men; you are to
bid any man stand, in the prince's name.

Sec. Watch.   How if a' will not stand?

Dog.   Why, then, take no note of him, but let him go; and presently call
the rest of the watch together, and thank God you are rid of a knave.

Verg.   If he will not stand when he is bidden, he is none of the
prince's subjects.

---

1. *senseless*] i.e., sensible.
2. *comprehend*] i.e., apprehend.
3. *vagrom*] i.e., vagrant.

DOG.   True, and they are to meddle with none but the prince's subjects. You shall also make no noise in the streets; for for the watch to
babble and to talk is most tolerable[4] and not to be endured.

WATCH.   We will rather sleep than talk: we know what belongs to a
watch.

DOG.   Why, you speak like an ancient and most quiet watchman; for I
cannot see how sleeping should offend: only, have a care that your
bills[5] be not stolen. Well, you are to call at all the ale-houses, and
bid those that are drunk get them to bed.

WATCH.   How if they will not?

DOG.   Why, then, let them alone till they are sober: if they make you
not then the better answer, you may say they are not the men you
took them for.

WATCH.   Well, sir.

DOG.   If you meet a thief, you may suspect him, by virtue of your
office, to be no true man; and, for such kind of men, the less you
meddle or make with them, why, the more is for your honesty.

WATCH.   If we know him to be a thief, shall we not lay hands on him?

DOG.   Truly, by your office, you may; but I think they that touch pitch
will be defiled: the most peaceable way for you, if you do take a thief,
is to let him show himself what he is, and steal out of your company.

VERG.   You have been always called a merciful man, partner.

DOG.   Truly, I would not hang a dog by my will, much more a man
who hath any honesty in him.

VERG.   If you hear a child cry in the night, you must call to the nurse
and bid her still it.

WATCH.   How if the nurse be asleep and will not hear us?

DOG.   Why, then, depart in peace, and let the child wake her with
crying; for the ewe that will not hear her lamb when it baes will
never answer a calf when he bleats.

VERG.   'Tis very true.

DOG.   This is the end of the charge:—you, constable, are to present
the prince's own person: if you meet the prince in the night, you
may stay him.

---

4. *tolerable*] i.e., intolerable.
5. *bills*] a kind of pike or halbert.

VERG.   Nay, by'r lady, that I think a' cannot.

DOG.   Five shillings to one on't, with any man that knows the statues, he may stay him: marry, not without the prince be willing; for, indeed, the watch ought to offend no man; and it is an offence to stay a man against his will.

VERG.   By'r lady, I think it be so.

DOG.   Ha, ah, ha! Well, masters, good night: an there be any matter of weight chances, call up me: keep your fellows' counsels and your own; and good night. Come, neighbour.

WATCH.   Well, masters, we hear our charge: let us go sit here upon the church-bench till two, and then all to bed.

DOG.   One word more, honest neighbours. I pray you, watch about Signior Leonato's door; for the wedding being there to-morrow, there is a great coil to-night. Adieu: be vigitant,[6] I beseech you.

[*Exeunt* DOGBERRY *and* VERGES.]

Enter BORACHIO *and* CONRADE.

BORA.   What, Conrade!

WATCH.   [*Aside*] Peace! stir not.

BORA.   Conrade, I say!

CON.   Here, man; I am at thy elbow.

BORA.   Mass, and my elbow itched; I thought there would a scab follow.

CON.   I will owe thee an answer for that: and now forward with thy tale.

BORA.   Stand thee close, then, under this pent-house, for it drizzles rain; and I will, like a true drunkard, utter all to thee.

WATCH.   [*Aside*] Some treason, masters: yet stand close.

BORA.   Therefore know I have earned of Don John a thousand ducats.

CON.   Is it possible that any villany should be so dear?

BORA.   Thou shouldst rather ask, if it were possible any villany should be so rich; for when rich villains have need of poor ones, poor ones may make what price they will.

CON.   I wonder at it.

BORA.   That shows thou art unconfirmed. Thou knowest that the fashion of a doublet, or a hat, or a cloak, is nothing to a man.

---

6. *vigitant*] i.e., vigilant.

CON.   Yes, it is apparel.

BORA.   I mean, the fashion.

CON.   Yes, the fashion is the fashion.

BORA.   Tush! I may as well say the fool's the fool. But seest thou not
what a deformed thief this fashion is?

WATCH. [*Aside*] I know that Deformed; a' has been a vile thief this
seven year; a' goes up and down like a gentleman: I remember his
name.

BORA.   Didst thou not hear somebody?

CON.   No; 'twas the vane on the house.

BORA.   Seest thou not, I say, what a deformed thief this fashion is?
how giddily a' turns about all the hot bloods between fourteen
and five-and-thirty? sometimes fashioning them like Pharaoh's
soldiers in the reechy[7] painting, sometime like god Bel's priests in
the old church-window, sometime like the shaven Hercules in the
smirched worm-eaten tapestry, where his codpiece seems as
massy as his club?

CON.   All this I see; and I see that the fashion wears out more apparel
than the man. But art not thou thyself giddy with the fashion too,
that thou hast shifted out of thy tale into telling me of the fashion?

BORA.   Not so, neither: but know that I have to-night wooed Margaret,
the Lady Hero's gentlewoman, by the name of Hero: she leans me
out at her mistress' chamber-window, bids me a thousand times good
night, —I tell this tale vilely: —I should first tell thee how the prince,
Claudio and my master, planted and placed and possessed by my
master Don John, saw afar off in the orchard this amiable encounter.

CON.   And thought they Margaret was Hero?

BORA.   Two of them did, the prince and Claudio; but the devil my
master knew she was Margaret; and partly by his oaths, which first
possessed them, partly by the dark night, which did deceive them,
but chiefly by my villany, which did confirm any slander that Don
John had made, away went Claudio enraged; swore he would meet
her, as he was appointed, next morning at the temple, and there,
before the whole congregation, shame her with what he saw o'er
night, and send her home again without a husband.

---

7. *reechy*] dirty, filthy.

FIRST WATCH.   We charge you, in the prince's name, stand!

SEC. WATCH.   Call up the right master constable. We have here recovered the most dangerous piece of lechery that ever was known in the commonwealth.

FIRST WATCH.   And one Deformed is one of them: I know him; a' wears a lock.[8]

CON.   Masters, masters,—

SEC. WATCH.   You'll be made bring Deformed forth, I warrant you.

CON.   Masters,—

FIRST WATCH.   Never speak: we charge you let us obey you to go with us.

BORA.   We are like to prove a goodly commodity, being taken up of these men's bills.

CON.   A commodity in question, I warrant you. Come, we'll obey you.

                                                                    [*Exeunt.*]

SCENE IV. HERO'S *apartment.*

Enter HERO, MARGARET, *and* URSULA.

HERO.   Good Ursula, wake my cousin Beatrice, and desire her to rise.

URS.   I will, lady.

HERO.   And bid her come hither.

URS.   Well.   [*Exit.*]

MARG.   Troth, I think your other rabato[1] were better.

HERO.   No, pray thee, good Meg, I'll wear this.

MARG.   By my troth's not so good; and I warrant your cousin will say so.

HERO.   My cousin's a fool, and thou art another: I'll wear none but this.

---

8. *lock*] a "love-lock": a ringlet of hair tied with a ribbon worn near the left ear by young men about town.

1. *rabato*] the word is used both for a ruff (stiff collar) and for the wire-support of the ruff.

MARG. I like the new tire[2] within excellently, if the hair were a thought browner; and your gown's a most rare fashion, i' faith. I saw the Duchess of Milan's gown that they praise so.

HERO. O, that exceeds, they say.

MARG. By my troth's but a night-gown in respect of yours,—cloth o' gold, and cuts, and laced with silver, set with pearls, down sleeves, side sleeves, and skirts, round underborne with a bluish tinsel: but for a fine, quaint, graceful and excellent fashion, yours is worth ten on't.

HERO. God give me joy to wear it! for my heart is exceeding heavy.

MARG. 'Twill be heavier soon by the weight of a man.

HERO. Fie upon thee! art not ashamed?

MARG. Of what, lady? of speaking honourably? Is not marriage honourable in a beggar? Is not your lord honourable without marriage? I think you would have me say, 'saving your reverence, a husband:' an bad thinking do not wrest true speaking, I'll offend nobody: is there any harm in 'the heavier for a husband'? None, I think, an it be the right husband and the right wife; otherwise 'tis light, and not heavy: ask my Lady Beatrice else; here she comes.

Enter BEATRICE.

HERO. Good morrow, coz.

BEAT. Good morrow, sweet Hero.

HERO. Why, how now? do you speak in the sick tune?

BEAT. I am out of all other tune, methinks.

MARG. Clap's into 'Light o' love;' that goes without a burden: do you sing it, and I'll dance it.

BEAT. Ye light o' love, with your heels! then, if your husband have stables enough, you'll see he shall lack no barns.

MARG. O illegitimate construction! I scorn that with my heels.

BEAT. 'Tis almost five o'clock, cousin; 'tis time you were ready. By my troth, I am exceeding ill: heigh-ho!

MARG. For a hawk, a horse, or a husband?

BEAT. For the letter that begins them all, H.

---

2. *tire*] headdress or cap to which false hair was attached.

MARG.   Well, an you be not turned Turk, there's no more sailing by the star.

BEAT.   What means the fool, trow?

MARG.   Nothing I; but God send every one their heart's desire!

HERO.   These gloves the count sent me; they are an excellent perfume.

BEAT.   I am stuffed, cousin; I cannot smell.

MARG.   A maid, and stuffed! there's goodly catching of cold.

BEAT.   O, God help me! God help me! how long have you professed apprehension?

MARG.   Ever since you left it. Doth not my wit become me rarely?

BEAT.   It is not seen enough, you should wear it in your cap. By my troth, I am sick.

MARG.   Get you some of this distilled Carduus Benedictus, and lay it to your heart: it is the only thing for a qualm.

HERO.   There thou prickest her with a thistle.

BEAT.   Benedictus! why Benedictus? you have some moral in this Benedictus.

MARG.   Moral! no, by my troth, I have no moral meaning; I meant, plain holy-thistle. You may think perchance that I think you are in love: nay, by'r lady, I am not such a fool to think what I list; nor I list not to think what I can; nor, indeed, I cannot think, if I would think my heart out of thinking, that you are in love, or that you will be in love, or that you can be in love. Yet Benedick was such another, and now is he become a man: he swore he would never marry; and yet now, in despite of his heart, he eats his meat without grudging: and how you may be converted, I know not; but methinks you look with your eyes as other women do.

BEAT.   What pace is this that thy tongue keeps?

MARG.   Not a false gallop.

Re-enter URSULA.

URS.   Madam, withdraw: the prince, the count, Signior Benedick, Don John, and all the gallants of the town, are come to fetch you to church.

HERO.   Help to dress me, good coz, good Meg, good Ursula. [*Exeunt.*]

SCENE V. *Another room in* LEONATO'S *house.*

Enter LEONATO, *with* DOGBERRY *and* VERGES.

LEON.   What would you with me, honest neighbour?

DOG.   Marry, sir, I would have some confidence[1] with you that de-cerns[2] you nearly.

LEON.   Brief, I pray you; for you see it is a busy time with me.

DOG.   Marry, this it is, sir.

VERG.   Yes, in truth it is, sir.

LEON.   What is it, my good friends?

DOG.   Goodman Verges, sir, speaks a little off the matter: an old man, sir, and his wits are not so blunt as, God help, I would desire they were; but, in faith, honest as the skin between his brows.

VERG.   Yes, I thank God I am as honest as any man living that is an old man and no honester than I.

DOG.   Comparisons are odorous:[3] palabras,[4] neighbour Verges.

LEON.   Neighbours, you are tedious.

DOG.   It pleases your worship to say so, but we are the poor duke's officers; but truly, for mine own part, if I were as tedious as a king, I could find in my heart to bestow it all of your worship.

LEON.   All thy tediousness on me, ah?

DOG.   Yea, an 'twere a thousand pound more than 'tis; for I hear as good exclamation[5] on your worship as of any man in the city; and though I be but a poor man, I am glad to hear it.

VERG.   And so am I.

LEON.   I would fain know what you have to say.

---

1. *confidence*] probably for "conference."
2. *decerns*] i.e., concerns.
3. *odorous*] i.e., odious.
4. *palabras*] *pocas palabras*, few words.
5. *exclamation*] possibly for "acclamation."

VERG. Marry, sir, our watch to-night, excepting your worship's presence, ha' ta'en a couple of as arrant knaves as any in Messina.

DOG. A good old man, sir; he will be talking: as they say, When the age is in, the wit is out: God help us! it is a world to see. Well said, i' faith, neighbour Verges: well, God's a good man; an two men ride of a horse, one must ride behind. An honest soul, i' faith, sir; by my troth he is, as ever broke bread; but God is to be worshipped; all men are not alike; alas, good neighbour!

LEON. Indeed, neighbour, he comes too short of you.

DOG. Gifts that God gives.

LEON. I must leave you.

DOG. One word, sir: our watch, sir, have indeed comprehended two aspicious[6] persons, and we would have them this morning examined before your worship.

LEON. Take their examination yourself, and bring it me: I am now in great haste, as it may appear unto you.

DOG. It shall be suffigance.[7]

LEON. Drink some wine ere you go: fare you well.

Enter a Messenger.

MESS. My lord, they stay for you to give your daughter to her husband.

LEON. I'll wait upon them: I am ready.

[*Exeunt* LEONATO *and* MESSENGER.]

DOG. Go, good partner, go, get you to Francis[8] Seacole; bid him bring his pen and inkhorn to the gaol: we are now to examination these men.

VERG. And we must do it wisely.

DOG. We will spare for no wit, I warrant you; here's that shall drive some of them to a noncome: only get the learned writer to set down our excommunication, and meet me at the gaol. [*Exeunt.*]

---

6. *aspicious*] i.e., suspicious.
7. *suffigance*] i.e., sufficient.
8. *Francis*] earlier, Seacole's first name is given as George (Act III, scene iii).

ACT IV.

SCENE I. *A church*.

Enter DON PEDRO, DON JOHN, LEONATO, FRIAR FRANCIS, CLAUDIO, BENEDICK, HERO, BEATRICE, *and* Attendants.

LEON. Come, Friar Francis, be brief; only to the plain form of marriage, and you shall recount their particular duties afterwards.

FRIAR. You come hither, my lord, to marry this lady.

CLAUD. No.

LEON. To be married to her: friar, you come to marry her.

FRIAR. Lady, you come hither to be married to this count.

HERO. I do.

FRIAR. If either of you know any inward impediment why you should not be conjoined, I charge you, on your souls, to utter it.

CLAUD. Know you any, Hero?

HERO. None, my lord.

FRIAR. Know you any, count?

LEON. I dare make his answer, none.

CLAUD. O, what men dare do! what men may do! what men daily do, not knowing what they do!

BENE. How now! interjections? Why, then, some be of laughing, as, ah, ha, he!

CLAUD. Stand thee by, friar. Father, by your leave:
Will you with free and unconstrained soul
Give me this maid, your daughter?

LEON. As freely, son, as God did give her me.

CLAUD. And what have I to give you back, whose worth
May counterpoise this rich and precious gift?

47

D. PEDRO.   Nothing, unless you render her again.

CLAUD.   Sweet prince, you learn me noble thankfulness.
    There, Leonato, take her back again:
    Give not this rotten orange to your friend;
    She's but the sign and semblance of her honour.
    Behold how like a maid she blushes here!
    O, what authority and show of truth
    Can cunning sin cover itself withal!
    Comes not that blood as modest evidence
    To witness simple virtue? Would you not swear,
    All you that see her, that she were a maid,
    By these exterior shows? But she is none:
    She knows the heat of a luxurious bed;
    Her blush is guiltiness, not modesty.

LEON.   What do you mean, my lord?

CLAUD.   Not to be married,
    Not to knit my soul to an approved wanton.

LEON.   Dear my lord, if you, in your own proof,
    Have vanquish'd the resistance of her youth,
    And made defeat of her virginity,—

CLAUD.   I know what you would say: if I have known her,
    You will say she did embrace me as a husband,
    And so extenuate the 'forehand sin:
    No, Leonato,
    I never tempted her with word too large;
    But, as a brother to his sister, show'd
    Bashful sincerity and comely love.

HERO.   And seem'd I ever otherwise to you?

CLAUD.   Out on thee! Seeming! I will write against it:
    You seem to me as Dian in her orb,
    As chaste as is the bud ere it be blown;
    But you are more intemperate in your blood
    Than Venus, or those pamper'd animals
    That rage in savage sensuality.

HERO.   Is my lord well, that he doth speak so wide?

LEON.   Sweet prince, why speak not you?

D. PEDRO.   What should I speak?
    I stand dishonour'd, that have gone about

To link my dear friend to a common stale.[1]

LEON. Are these things spoken, or do I but dream?

D. JOHN. Sir, they are spoken, and these things are true.

BENE. This looks not like a nuptial.

HERO.   True! O God!

CLAUD. Leonato, stand I here?
   Is this the prince? is this the prince's brother?
   Is this face Hero's? are our eyes our own?

LEON. All this is so: but what of this, my lord?

CLAUD. Let me but move one question to your daughter;
   And, by that fatherly and kindly power
   That you have in her, bid her answer truly.

LEON. I charge thee do so, as thou art my child.

HERO. O, God defend me! how am I beset!
   What kind of catechising call you this?

CLAUD. To make you answer truly to your name.

HERO. Is it not Hero? Who can blot that name
   With any just reproach?

CLAUD.   Marry, that can Hero;
   Hero itself can blot out Hero's virtue.
   What man was he talk'd with you yesternight
   Out at your window betwixt twelve and one?
   Now, if you are a maid, answer to this.

HERO. I talk'd with no man at that hour, my lord.

D. PEDRO. Why, then are you no maiden. Leonato,
   I am sorry you must hear: upon mine honour,
   Myself, my brother, and this grieved count
   Did see her, hear her, at that hour last night
   Talk with a ruffian at her chamber-window;
   Who hath indeed, most like a liberal villain,
   Confess'd the vile encounters they have had
   A thousand times in secret.

D. JOHN. Fie, fie! they are not to be named, my lord,
   Not to be spoke of;

---

1. *stale*] something worn out by use; i.e., a prostitute.

There is not chastity enough in language,
Without offence to utter them. Thus, pretty lady,
I am sorry for thy much misgovernment.

CLAUD.   O Hero, what a Hero hadst thou been,
If half thy outward graces had been placed
About thy thoughts and counsels of thy heart!
But fare thee well, most foul, most fair! farewell,
Thou pure impiety and impious purity!
For thee I'll lock up all the gates of love,
And on my eyelids shall conjecture hang,
To turn all beauty into thoughts of harm,
And never shall it more be gracious.

LEON.   Hath no man's dagger here a point for me?   [HERO *swoons.*]

BEAT.   Why, how now, cousin! wherefore sink you down?

D. JOHN.   Come, let us go. These things, come thus to light,
Smother her spirits up.

> *[Exeunt* DON PEDRO, DON JOHN, *and* CLAUDIO.]

BENE.   How doth the lady?

BEAT.   Dead, I think. Help, uncle!
Hero! why, Hero! Uncle! Signior Benedick! Friar!

LEON.   O Fate! take not away thy heavy hand.
Death is the fairest cover for her shame
That may be wish'd for.

BEAT.   How now, cousin Hero!

FRIAR.   Have comfort, lady.

LEON.   Dost thou look up?

FRIAR.   Yea, wherefore should she not?

LEON.   Wherefore! Why, doth not every earthly thing
Cry shame upon her? Could she here deny
The story that is printed in her blood?
Do not live, Hero; do not ope thine eyes:
For, did I think thou wouldst not quickly die,
Thought I thy spirits were stronger than thy shames,
Myself would, on the rearward of reproaches,
Strike at thy life. Grieved I, I had but one?
Chid I for that at frugal nature's frame?
O, one too much by thee! Why had I one?
Why ever wast thou lovely in my eyes?

Why had I not with charitable hand
Took up a beggar's issue at my gates,
Who smirched thus and mired with infamy,
I might have said, 'No part of it is mine;
This shame derives itself from unknown loins'?
But mine, and mine I loved, and mine I praised,
And mine that I was proud on, mine so much
That I myself was to myself not mine,
Valuing of her,—why, she, O, she is fallen
Into a pit of ink, that the wide sea
Hath drops too few to wash her clean again,
And salt too little which may season give
To her foul-tainted flesh!

BENE.   Sir, sir, be patient.
For my part, I am so attired in wonder,
I know not what to say.

BEAT.   O, on my soul, my cousin is belied!

BENE.   Lady, were you her bedfellow last night?

BEAT.   No, truly, not; although, until last night,
I have this twelvemonth been her bedfellow.

LEON.   Confirm'd, confirm'd! O, that is stronger made
Which was before barr'd up with ribs of iron!
Would the two princes lie, and Claudio lie,
Who loved her so, that, speaking of her foulness,
Wash'd it with tears? Hence from her! let her die.

FRIAR.   Hear me a little;
For I have only been silent so long,
And given way unto this course of fortune,
By noting of the lady: I have mark'd
A thousand blushing apparitions
To start into her face; a thousand innocent shames
In angel whiteness beat away those blushes;
And in her eye there hath appear'd a fire,
To burn the errors that these princes hold
Against her maiden truth. Call me a fool;
Trust not my reading nor my observations,
Which with experimental seal doth warrant
The tenour of my book; trust not my age,

My reverence, calling, nor divinity,
If this sweet lady lie not guiltless here
Under some biting error.

LEON.   Friar, it cannot be.
Thou seest that all the grace that she hath left
Is that she will not add to her damnation
A sin of perjury; she not denies it:
Why seek'st thou, then, to cover with excuse
That which appears in proper nakedness?

FRIAR.   Lady, what man is he you are accused of?

HERO.   They know that do accuse me; I know none:
If I know more of any man alive
Than that which maiden modesty doth warrant,
Let all my sins lack mercy! O my father,
Prove you that any man with me conversed
At hours unmeet, or that I yesternight
Maintain'd the change of words with any creature,
Refuse me, hate me, torture me to death!

FRIAR.   There is some strange misprision in the princes.

BENE.   Two of them have the very bent of honour;
And if their wisdoms be misled in this,
The practice of it lives in John the bastard,
Whose spirits toil in frame of villanies.

LEON.   I know not. If they speak but truth of her,
These hands shall tear her; if they wrong her honour,
The proudest of them shall well hear of it.
Time hath not yet so dried this blood of mine,
Nor age so eat up my invention,
Nor fortune made such havoc of my means,
Nor my bad life reft me so much of friends,
But they shall find, awaked in such a kind,
Both strength of limb and policy of mind,
Ability in means and choice of friends,
To quit me of them thoroughly.

FRIAR.   Pause awhile,
And let my counsel sway you in this case.
Your daughter here the princes left for dead:
Let her awhile be secretly kept in,

And publish it that she is dead indeed;
Maintain a mourning ostentation,
And on your family's old monument
Hang mournful epitaphs, and do all rites
That appertain unto a burial.

LEON.   What shall become of this? what will this do?

FRIAR.   Marry, this, well carried, shall on her behalf
Change slander to remorse; that is some good:
But not for that dream I on this strange course,
But on this travail look for greater birth.
She dying, as it must be so maintain'd,
Upon the instant that she was accused,
Shall be lamented, pitied, and excused
Of every hearer: for it so falls out,
That what we have we prize not to the worth
Whiles we enjoy it; but being lack'd and lost,
Why, then we rack the value, then we find
The virtue that possession would not show us
Whiles it was ours. So will it fare with Claudio:
When he shall hear she died upon his words,
The idea of her life shall sweetly creep
Into his study of imagination;
And every lovely organ of her life
Shall come apparell'd in more precious habit,
More moving-delicate and full of life,
Into the eye and prospect of his soul,
Than when she lived indeed; then shall he mourn,
If ever love had interest in his liver,
And wish he had not so accused her,
No, though he thought his accusation true.
Let this be so, and doubt not but success
Will fashion the event in better shape
Than I can lay it down in likelihood.
But if all aim but this be levell'd false,
The supposition of the lady's death
Will quench the wonder of her infamy:
And if it sort not well, you may conceal her,
As best befits her wounded reputation,

In some reclusive and religious life,
Out of all eyes, tongues, minds, and injuries.

BENE.   Signior Leonato, let the friar advise you:
And though you know my inwardness and love
Is very much unto the prince and Claudio,
Yet, by mine honour, I will deal in this
As secretly and justly as your soul
Should with your body.

LEON.   Being that I flow in grief,
The smallest twine may lead me.

FRIAR.   'Tis well consented: presently away;
For to strange sores strangely they strain the cure.
Come, lady, die to live: this wedding-day
Perhaps is but prolong'd: have patience and endure.

[*Exeunt all but* BENEDICK *and* BEATRICE.]

BENE.   Lady Beatrice, have you wept all this while?

BEAT.   Yea, and I will weep a while longer.

BENE.   I will not desire that.

BEAT.   You have no reason; I do it freely.

BENE.   Surely I do believe your fair cousin is wronged.

BEAT.   Ah, how much might the man deserve of me that would right her!

BENE.   Is there any way to show such friendship?

BEAT.   A very even way, but no such friend.

BENE.   May a man do it?

BEAT.   It is a man's office, but not yours.

BENE.   I do love nothing in the world so well as you: is not that strange?

BEAT.   As strange as the thing I know not. It were as possible for me to say I loved nothing so well as you: but believe me not; and yet I lie not; I confess nothing, nor I deny nothing. I am sorry for my cousin.

BENE.   By my sword, Beatrice, thou lovest me.

BEAT.   Do not swear, and eat it.

BENE.   I will swear by it that you love me; and I will make him eat it that says I love not you.

BEAT.   Will you not eat your word?

BENE.   With no sauce that can be devised to it. I protest I love thee.

BEAT.   Why, then, God forgive me!

BENE.   What offence, sweet Beatrice?

BEAT.   You have stayed me in a happy hour: I was about to protest I loved you.

BENE.   And do it with all thy heart.

BEAT.   I love you with so much of my heart, that none is left to protest.

BENE.   Come, bid me do any thing for thee.

BEAT.   Kill Claudio.

BENE.   Ha! not for the wide world.

BEAT.   You kill me to deny it. Farewell.

BENE.   Tarry, sweet Beatrice.

BEAT.   I am gone, though I am here: there is no love in you: nay, I pray you, let me go.

BENE.   Beatrice,—

BEAT.   In faith, I will go.

BENE.   We'll be friends first.

BEAT.   You dare easier be friends with me than fight with mine enemy.

BENE.   Is Claudio thine enemy?

BEAT.   Is he not approved in the height a villain, that hath slandered, scorned, dishonoured my kinswoman? O that I were a man! What, bear her in hand until they come to take hands; and then, with public accusation, uncovered slander, unmitigated rancour,—O God, that I were a man! I would eat his heart in the market-place.

BENE.   Hear me, Beatrice,—

BEAT.   Talk with a man out at a window! A proper saying!

BENE.   Nay, but, Beatrice,—

BEAT.   Sweet Hero! She is wronged, she is slandered, she is undone.

BENE.   Beat—

BEAT.   Princes and counties! Surely, a princely testimony, a goodly count, Count Comfect;[2] a sweet gallant, surely! O that I were a man for his sake! or that I had any friend would be a man for my sake! But manhood is melted into courtesies, valour into compliment, and men are only turned into tongue, and trim ones too: he is now as valiant as Hercules that only tells a lie, and swears it. I cannot be a man with wishing, therefore I will die a woman with grieving.

BENE.   Tarry, good Beatrice. By this hand, I love thee.

---

2. *Count Comfect*] a sugar-plum count; "comfect" is the same as "comfit," a sweetmeat.

BEAT. Use it for my love some other way than swearing by it.

BENE. Think you in your soul the Count Claudio hath wronged
Hero?

BEAT. Yea, as sure as I have a thought or a soul.

BENE. Enough, I am engaged; I will challenge him. I will kiss your
hand, and so I leave you. By this hand, Claudio shall render me a
dear account. As you hear of me, so think of me. Go, comfort your
cousin: I must say she is dead: and so, farewell. [*Exeunt.*]

SCENE II. *A prison.*

Enter DOGBERRY, VERGES, *and* Sexton, *in gowns; and the* Watch, *with*
CONRADE *and* BORACHIO.

DOG. Is our whole dissembly[1] appeared?

VERG. O, a stool and a cushion for the sexton.

SEX. Which be the malefactors?

DOG. Marry, that am I and my partner.

VERG. Nay, that's certain; we have the exhibition to examine.

SEX. But which are the offenders that are to be examined? let them
come before master constable.

DOG. Yea, marry, let them come before me. What is your name,
friend?

BORA. Borachio.

DOG. Pray, write down, Borachio. Yours, sirrah?

CON. I am a gentleman, sir, and my name is Conrade.

DOG. Write down, master gentleman Conrade. Masters, do you serve
God?

CON.⎫
BORA.⎭ Yea, sir, we hope.

---

1. *dissembly*] i.e., assembly.

DOG.   Write down, that they hope they serve God: and write God first; for God defend but God should go before such villains! Masters, it is proved already that you are little better than false knaves; and it will go near to be thought so shortly. How answer you for yourselves?

CON.   Marry, sir, we say we are none.

DOG.   A marvellous witty fellow, I assure you; but I will go about with him. Come you hither, sirrah; a word in your ear: sir, I say to you, it is thought you are false knaves.

BORA.   Sir, I say to you we are none.

DOG.   Well, stand aside. 'Fore God, they are both in a tale. Have you writ down, that they are none?

SEX.   Master constable, you go not the way to examine: you must call forth the watch that are their accusers.

DOG.   Yea, marry, that's the eftest[2] way. Let the watch come forth. Masters, I charge you, in the prince's name, accuse these men.

FIRST WATCH.   This man said, sir, that Don John, the prince's brother, was a villain.

DOG.   Write down, Prince John a villain. Why, this is flat perjury, to call a prince's brother villain.

BORA.   Master constable,—

DOG.   Pray thee, fellow, peace: I do not like thy look, I promise thee.

SEX.   What heard you him say else?

SEC. WATCH.   Marry, that he had received a thousand ducats of Don John for accusing the Lady Hero wrongfully.

DOG.   Flat burglary as ever was committed.

VERG.   Yea, by mass, that it is.

SEX.   What else, fellow?

FIRST WATCH.   And that Count Claudio did mean, upon his words, to disgrace Hero before the whole assembly, and not marry her.

DOG.   O villain! thou wilt be condemned into everlasting redemption[3] for this.

SEX.   What else?

WATCH.   This is all.

---

2. *eftest*] the meaning is uncertain; possibly Dogberry's word for easiest.

3. *redemption*] i.e., perdition.

SEX.   And this is more, masters, than you can deny. Prince John is this
        morning secretly stolen away; Hero was in this manner accused, in
        this very manner refused, and upon the grief of this suddenly died.
        Master constable, let these men be bound, and brought to
        Leonato's: I will go before and show him their examination. [*Exit.*]
DOG.   Come, let them be opinioned.[4]
VERG.   Let them be in the hands—
CON.   Off, coxcomb!
DOG.   God's my life, where's the sexton? let him write down, the
        prince's officer, coxcomb. Come, bind them. Thou naughty varlet!
CON.   Away! you are an ass, you are an ass.
DOG.   Dost thou not suspect[5] my place? dost thou not suspect my
        years? O that he were here to write me down an ass! But, masters,
        remember that I am an ass; though it be not written down, yet
        forget not that I am an ass. No, thou villain, thou art full of piety,[6] as
        shall be proved upon thee by good witness. I am a wise fellow; and,
        which is more, an officer; and, which is more, a householder; and,
        which is more, as pretty a piece of flesh as any is in Messina; and
        one that knows the law, go to; and a rich fellow enough, go to; and a
        fellow that hath had losses; and one that hath two gowns, and every
        thing handsome about him. Bring him away. O that I had been writ
        down an ass!   [*Exeunt.*]

---

4. *opinioned*] i.e., pinioned.
5. *suspect*] i.e., respect.
6. *piety*] i.e., impiety.

ACT V.

Scene I. *Before* Leonato's *house*.

Enter Leonato *and* Antonio.

ANT. If you go on thus, you will kill yourself;
  And 'tis not wisdom thus to second grief
  Against yourself.
LEON.   I pray thee, cease thy counsel,
  Which falls into mine ears as profitless
  As water in a sieve: give not me counsel;
  Nor let no comforter delight mine ear
  But such a one whose wrongs do suit with mine.
  Bring me a father that so loved his child,
  Whose joy of her is overwhelm'd like mine,
  And bid him speak of patience;
  Measure his woe the length and breadth of mine,
  And let it answer every strain for strain,
  As thus for thus, and such a grief for such,
  In every lineament, branch, shape, and form:
  If such a one will smile, and stroke his beard,
  Bid sorrow wag, cry 'hem!' when he should groan,
  Patch grief with proverbs, make misfortune drunk
  With candle-wasters; bring him yet to me,
  And I of him will gather patience.
  But there is no such man: for, brother, men
  Can counsel and speak comfort to that grief
  Which they themselves not feel; but, tasting it,
  Their counsel turns to passion, which before
  Would give preceptial medicine to rage,

Fetter strong madness in a silken thread,
Charm ache with air, and agony with words:
No, no; 'tis all men's office to speak patience
To those that wring under the load of sorrow,
But no man's virtue nor sufficiency,
To be so moral when he shall endure
The like himself. Therefore give me no counsel:
My griefs cry louder than advertisement.
ANT.   Therein do men from children nothing differ.
LEON.   I pray thee, peace. I will be flesh and blood;
For there was never yet philosopher
That could endure the toothache patiently,
However they have writ the style of gods,
And made a push at chance and sufferance.
ANT.   Yet bend not all the harm upon yourself;
Make those that do offend you suffer too.
LEON.   There thou speak'st reason: nay, I will do so.
My soul doth tell me Hero is belied;
And that shall Claudio know; so shall the prince,
And all of them that thus dishonour her.
ANT.   Here comes the prince and Claudio hastily.

Enter DON PEDRO *and* CLAUDIO.

D. PEDRO.   Good den, good den.
CLAUD.   Good day to both of you.
LEON.   Hear you, my lords,—
D. PEDRO.   We have some haste, Leonato.
LEON.   Some haste, my lord! well, fare you well, my lord:
Are you so hasty now? well, all is one.
D. PEDRO.   Nay, do not quarrel with us, good old man.
ANT.   If he could right himself with quarrelling,
Some of us would lie low.
CLAUD.   Who wrongs him?
LEON.   Marry, thou dost wrong me, thou dissembler, thou:—
Nay, never lay thy hand upon thy sword;
I fear thee not.
CLAUD.   Marry, beshrew my hand,
If it should give your age such cause of fear:

    In faith, my hand meant nothing to my sword.

LEON.   Tush, tush, man; never fleer and jest at me:
    I speak not like a dotard nor a fool,
    As, under privilege of age, to brag
    What I have done being young, or what would do,
    Were I not old. Know, Claudio, to thy head,
    Thou hast so wrong'd mine innocent child and me,
    That I am forced to lay my reverence by,
    And, with grey hairs and bruise of many days,
    Do challenge thee to trial of a man.
    I say thou hast belied mine innocent child;
    Thy slander hath gone through and through her heart,
    And she lies buried with her ancestors;
    O, in a tomb where never scandal slept,
    Save this of hers, framed by thy villany!

CLAUD.   My villany?

LEON.   Thine, Claudio; thine, I say.

D. PEDRO.   You say not right, old man.

LEON.   My lord, my lord,
    I'll prove it on his body, if he dare,
    Despite his nice fence and his active practice,
    His May of youth and bloom of lustihood.

CLAUD.   Away! I will not have to do with you.

LEON.   Canst thou so daff me? Thou hast kill'd my child:
    If thou kill'st me, boy, thou shalt kill a man.

ANT.   He shall kill two of us, and men indeed:
    But that's no matter; let him kill one first;
    Win me and wear me; let him answer me.
    Come, follow me, boy; come, sir boy, come, follow me:
    Sir boy, I'll whip you from your foining[1] fence;
    Nay, as I am a gentleman, I will.

LEON.   Brother,—

ANT.   Content yourself. God knows I loved my niece;
    And she is dead, slander'd to death by villains,
    That dare as well answer a man indeed

---

1. *foining*] thrusting.

As I dare take a serpent by the tongue:
Boys, apes, braggarts, Jacks, milksops!

LEON.   Brother Antony,—

ANT.   Hold you content. What, man! I know them, yea,
And what they weigh, even to the utmost scruple,—
Scambling, out-facing, fashion-monging boys,
That lie, and cog, and flout, deprave, and slander,
Go antiquely, and show outward hideousness,
And speak off half a dozen dangerous words,
How they might hurt their enemies, if they durst;
And this is all.

LEON.   But, brother Antony,—

ANT.   Come, 'tis no matter:
Do not you meddle; let me deal in this.

D. PEDRO.   Gentlemen both, we will not wake your patience.
My heart is sorry for your daughter's death:
But, on my honour, she was charged with nothing
But what was true, and very full of proof.

LEON.   My lord, my lord,—

D. PEDRO.   I will not hear you.

LEON.   No? Come, brother; away! I will be heard.

ANT.   And shall, or some of us will smart for it.

                        [*Exeunt* LEONATO *and* ANTONIO.]

D. PEDRO.   See, see; here comes the man we went to seek.

Enter BENEDICK.

CLAUD.   Now, signior, what news?

BENE.   Good day, my lord.

D. PEDRO.   Welcome, signior: you are almost come to part almost a
fray.

CLAUD.   We had like to have had our two noses snapped off with two
old men without teeth.

D. PEDRO.   Leonato and his brother. What thinkest thou? Had we
fought, I doubt we should have been too young for them.

BENE.   In a false quarrel there is no true valour. I came to seek you both.

CLAUD.   We have been up and down to seek thee; for we are high-
proof melancholy, and would fain have it beaten away. Wilt thou
use thy wit?

BENE.   It is in my scabbard: shall I draw it?

D. PEDRO.   Dost thou wear thy wit by thy side?

CLAUD.   Never any did so, though very many have been beside their wit. I will bid thee draw, as we do the minstrels; draw, to pleasure us.

D. PEDRO.   As I am an honest man, he looks pale. Art thou sick, or angry?

CLAUD.   What, courage, man! What though care killed a cat, thou hast mettle enough in thee to kill care.

BENE.   Sir, I shall meet your wit in the career, an you charge it against me. I pray you choose another subject.

CLAUD.   Nay, then, give him another staff: this last was broke cross.

D. PEDRO.   By this light, he changes more and more: I think he be angry indeed.

CLAUD.   If he be, he knows how to turn his girdle.

BENE.   Shall I speak a word in your ear?

CLAUD.   God bless me from a challenge!

BENE.   [*Aside to* CLAUDIO] You are a villain; I jest not: I will make it good how you dare, with what you dare, and when you dare. Do me right, or I will protest your cowardice. You have killed a sweet lady, and her death shall fall heavy on you. Let me hear from you.

CLAUD.   Well, I will meet you, so I may have good cheer.

D. PEDRO.   What, a feast, a feast?

CLAUD.   I'faith, I thank him; he hath bid me to a calf's-head and a capon; the which if I do not carve most curiously, say my knife's naught. Shall I not find a woodcock too?

BENE.   Sir, your wit ambles well; it goes easily.

D. PEDRO.   I'll tell thee how Beatrice praised thy wit the other day. I said, thou hadst a fine wit: 'True,' said she, 'a fine little one.' 'No,' said I, 'a great wit:' 'Right,' says she, 'a great gross one.' 'Nay,' said I, 'a good wit:' 'Just,' said she, 'it hurts nobody.' 'Nay,' said I, 'the gentleman is wise:' 'Certain,' said she, 'a wise gentleman.' 'Nay,' said I, 'he hath the tongues:' 'That I believe,' said she, 'for he swore a thing to me on Monday night, which he forswore on Tuesday morning; there's a double tongue; there's two tongues.' Thus did she, an hour together, trans-shape thy particular virtues: yet at last she concluded with a sigh, thou wast the properest man in Italy.

CLAUD.   For the which she wept heartily, and said she cared not.

D. PEDRO.   Yea, that she did; but yet, for all that, an if she did not hate him deadly, she would love him dearly: the old man's daughter told us all.

CLAUD.   All, all; and, moreover, God saw him when he was hid in the garden.

D. PEDRO.   But when shall we set the savage bull's horns on the sensible Benedick's head?

CLAUD.   Yea, and text underneath, 'Here dwells Benedick the married man'?

BENE.   Fare you well, boy: you know my mind. I will leave you now to your gossip-like humour: you break jests as braggarts do their blades, which, God be thanked, hurt not. My lord, for your many courtesies I thank you: I must discontinue your company: your brother the bastard is fled from Messina: you have among you killed a sweet and innocent lady. For my Lord Lackbeard there, he and I shall meet: and till then peace be with him.   [*Exit.*]

D. PEDRO.   He is in earnest.

CLAUD.   In most profound earnest; and, I'll warrant you, for the love of Beatrice.

D. PEDRO.   And hath challenged thee.

CLAUD.   Most sincerely.

D. PEDRO.   What a pretty thing man is when he goes in his doublet and hose, and leaves off his wit!

CLAUD.   He is then a giant to an ape: but then is an ape a doctor to such a man.

D. PEDRO.   But, soft you, let me be: pluck up, my heart, and be sad. Did he not say, my brother was fled?

Enter DOGBERRY, VERGES, *and the* Watch, *with* CONRADE *and* BO-RACHIO.

DOG.   Come, you, sir: if justice cannot tame you, she shall ne'er weigh more reasons in her balance: nay, an you be a cursing hypocrite once, you must be looked to.

D. PEDRO.   How now? two of my brother's men bound! Borachio one!

CLAUD.   Hearken after their offence, my lord.

D. PEDRO.   Officers, what offence have these men done?

DOG.   Marry, sir, they have committed false report; moreover, they have spoken untruths; secondarily, they are slanders; sixth and

lastly, they have belied a lady; thirdly, they have verified unjust
things; and, to conclude, they are lying knaves.

D. PEDRO.   First, I ask thee what they have done; thirdly, I ask thee
what's their offence; sixth and lastly, why they are committed; and,
to conclude, what you lay to their charge.

CLAUD.   Rightly reasoned, and in his own division; and, by my troth,
there's one meaning well suited.

D. PEDRO.   Who have you offended, masters, that you are thus bound
to your answer? this learned constable is too cunning to be under-
stood: what's your offence?

BORA.   Sweet prince, let me go no farther to mine answer: do you hear
me, and let this count kill me. I have deceived even your very eyes:
what your wisdoms could not discover, these shallow fools have
brought to light; who, in the night, overheard me confessing to this
man, how Don John your brother incensed me to slander the Lady
Hero; how you were brought into the orchard, and saw me court
Margaret in Hero's garments: how you disgraced her, when you
should marry her: my villany they have upon record; which I had
rather seal with my death than repeat over to my shame. The lady is
dead upon mine and my master's false accusation; and, briefly, I
desire nothing but the reward of a villain.

D. PEDRO.   Runs not this speech like iron through your blood?

CLAUD.   I have drunk poison whiles he utter'd it.

D. PEDRO.   But did my brother set thee on to this?

BORA.   Yea, and paid me richly for the practice of it.

D. PEDRO.   He is composed and framed of treachery:
And fled he is upon this villany.

CLAUD.   Sweet Hero! now thy image doth appear
In the rare semblance that I loved it first.

DOG.   Come, bring away the plaintiffs: by this time our sexton
hath reformed² Signior Leonato of the matter: and, masters, do
not forget to specify, when time and place shall serve, that I am an
ass.

VERG.   Here, here comes master Signior Leonato, and the sexton
too.

---

2. *reformed*] i.e., informed.

Re-enter LEONATO *and* ANTONIO, *with the* Sexton.

LEON.   Which is the villain? let me see his eyes,
    That, when I note another man like him,
    I may avoid him: which of these is he?
BORA.   If you would know your wronger, look on me.
LEON.   Art thou the slave that with thy breath hast kill'd
    Mine innocent child?
BORA.   Yea, even I alone.
LEON.   No, not so, villain; thou beliest thyself:
    Here stand a pair of honourable men;
    A third is fled, that had a hand in it.
    I thank you, princes, for my daughter's death:
    Record it with your high and worthy deeds:
    'Twas bravely done, if you bethink you of it.
CLAUD.   I know not how to pray your patience;
    Yet I must speak. Choose your revenge yourself;
    Impose me to what penance your invention
    Can lay upon my sin: yet sinn'd I not
    But in mistaking.
D. PEDRO.   By my soul, nor I:
    And yet, to satisfy this good old man,
    I would bend under any heavy weight
    That he'll enjoin me to.
LEON.   I cannot bid you bid my daughter live;
    That were impossible: but, I pray you both,
    Possess[3] the people in Messina here
    How innocent she died; and if your love
    Can labour aught in sad invention,
    Hang her an epitaph upon her tomb,
    And sing it to her bones, sing it to-night:
    To-morrow morning come you to my house;
    And since you could not be my son-in-law,
    Be yet my nephew: my brother hath a daughter,
    Almost the copy of my child that's dead,

---

3. *Possess*] inform.

And she alone is heir to both of us:
Give her the right you should have given her cousin,
And so dies my revenge.

CLAUD.   O noble sir,
Your over-kindness doth wring tears from me!
I do embrace your offer; and dispose
For henceforth of poor Claudio.

LEON.   To-morrow, then, I will expect your coming;
To-night I take my leave. This naughty man
Shall face to face be brought to Margaret,
Who I believe was pack'd in all this wrong,
Hired to it by your brother.

BORA.   No, by my soul, she was not;
Nor knew not what she did when she spoke to me;
But always hath been just and virtuous
In any thing that I do know by her.

DOG.   Moreover, sir, which indeed is not under white and black, this
plaintiff here, the offender, did call me ass: I beseech you, let it be
remembered in his punishment. And also, the watch heard them
talk of one Deformed: they say he wears a key in his ear, and a lock
hanging by it; and borrows money in God's name, the which he
hath used so long and never paid, that now men grow hard-hearted,
and will lend nothing for God's sake: pray you, examine him upon
that point.

LEON.   I thank thee for thy care and honest pains.

DOG.   Your worship speaks like a most thankful and reverend youth;
and I praise God for you.

LEON.   There's for thy pains.

DOG.   God save the foundation!

LEON.   Go, I discharge thee of thy prisoner, and I thank thee.

DOG.   I leave an arrant knave with your worship; which I beseech your
worship to correct yourself, for the example of others. God keep
your worship! I wish your worship well; God restore you to health! I
humbly give you leave to depart; and if a merry meeting may be
wished, God prohibit it! Come, neighbour.

                              [*Exeunt* DOGBERRY *and* VERGES.]

LEON.   Until to-morrow morning, lords, farewell.

ANT.   Farewell, my lords: we look for you to-morrow.

D. Pedro.   We will not fail.

Claud.   To-night I'll mourn with Hero.

Leon.   [*To the* Watch] Bring you these fellows on. We'll talk with Margaret,

How her acquaintance grew with this lewd fellow.

[*Exeunt, severally.*]

SCENE II. LEONATO'S *garden*.

Enter BENEDICK *and* MARGARET, *meeting*.

Bene.   Pray thee, sweet Mistress Margaret, deserve well at my hands by helping me to the speech of Beatrice.

Marg.   Will you, then, write me a sonnet in praise of my beauty?

Bene.   In so high a style, Margaret, that no man living shall come over it; for, in most comely truth, thou deservest it.

Marg.   To have no man come over me! why, shall I always keep below stairs?

Bene.   Thy wit is as quick as the greyhound's mouth; it catches.

Marg.   And yours as blunt as the fencer's foils, which hit, but hurt not.

Bene.   A most manly wit, Margaret; it will not hurt a woman: and so, I pray thee, call Beatrice: I give thee the bucklers.

Marg.   Give us the swords; we have bucklers of our own.

Bene.   If you use them, Margaret, you must put in the pikes with a vice; and they are dangerous weapons for maids.

Marg.   Well, I will call Beatrice to you, who I think hath legs.

Bene.   And therefore will come.   [*Exit* MARGARET.]

[*Sings*]   The god of love,
                              That sits above,
                    And knows me, and knows me,
                       How pitiful I deserve,—

I mean in singing; but in loving, Leander the good swimmer,

Troilus the first employer of pandars, and a whole bookful of these quondam carpet-mongers, whose names yet run smoothly in the even road of a blank verse, why, they were never so truly turned over and over as my poor self in love. Marry, I cannot show it in rhyme; I have tried: I can find out no rhyme to 'lady' but 'baby,' an innocent rhyme; for 'scorn,' 'horn,' a hard rhyme; for 'school,' 'fool,' a babbling rhyme; very ominous endings: no, I was not born under a rhyming planet, nor I cannot woo in festival terms.

Enter BEATRICE.

Sweet Beatrice, wouldst thou come when I called thee?

BEAT.   Yea, signior, and depart when you bid me.

BENE.   O, stay but till then!

BEAT.   'Then' is spoken; fare you well now: and yet, ere I go, let me go with that I came; which is, with knowing what hath passed between you and Claudio.

BENE.   Only foul words; and thereupon I will kiss thee.

BEAT.   Foul words is but foul wind, and foul wind is but foul breath, and foul breath is noisome; therefore I will depart unkissed.

BENE.   Thou has frighted the word out of his right sense, so forcible is thy wit. But I must tell thee plainly, Claudio undergoes my challenge; and either I must shortly hear from him, or I will subscribe him a coward. And, I pray thee now, tell me for which of my bad parts didst thou first fall in love with me?

BEAT.   For them all together; which maintained so politic a state of evil, that they will not admit any good part to intermingle with them. But for which of my good parts did you first suffer love for me?

BENE.   Suffer love,—a good epithet! I do suffer love indeed, for I love thee against my will.

BEAT.   In spite of your heart, I think; alas, poor heart! If you spite it for my sake, I will spite it for yours; for I will never love that which my friend hates.

BENE.   Thou and I are too wise to woo peaceably.

BEAT.   It appears not in this confession: there's not one wise man among twenty that will praise himself.

BENE.   An old, an old instance, Beatrice, that lived in the time of good neighbours. If a man do not erect in this age his own tomb ere he dies, he shall live no longer in monument than the bell rings and the widow weeps.

BEAT. And how long is that, think you?

BENE. Question: why, an hour in clamour, and a quarter in rheum: therefore is it most expedient for the wise, if Don Worm, his conscience, find no impediment to the contrary, to be the trumpet of his own virtues, as I am to myself. So much for praising myself, who, I myself will bear witness, is praiseworthy: and now tell me, how doth your cousin?

BEAT. Very ill.

BENE. And how do you?

BEAT. Very ill too.

BENE. Serve God, love me, and mend. There will I leave you too, for here comes one in haste.

Enter URSULA.

URS. Madam, you must come to your uncle. Yonder's old coil at home: it is proved my Lady Hero hath been falsely accused, the prince and Claudio mightily abused; and Don John is the author of all, who is fled and gone. Will you come presently?

BEAT. Will you go hear this news, signior?

BENE. I will live in thy heart, die in thy lap, and be buried in thy eyes; and moreover I will go with thee to thy uncle's.   [*Exeunt.*]

SCENE III. A *church*.

Enter DON PEDRO, CLAUDIO, *and three or four with tapers.*

CLAUD. Is this the monument of Leonato?

A LORD. It is, my lord.

CLAUD. [*Reading out of a scroll*]

Done to death by slanderous tongues
　Was the Hero that here lies:
Death, in guerdon[1] of her wrongs,
　Gives her fame which never dies.
So the life that died with shame
Lives in death with glorious fame.

Hang thou there upon the tomb,
Praising her when I am dumb.
Now, music, sound, and sing your solemn hymn.

SONG.

Pardon, goddess of the night,
Those that slew thy virgin knight;
For the which, with songs of woe,
Round about her tomb they go.
　Midnight, assist our moan;
　Help us to sigh and groan,
　　Heavily, heavily:
Graves, yawn, and yield your dead,
Till death be uttered,
　　Heavily, heavily.

CLAUD.   Now, unto thy bones good night!
　　Yearly will I do this rite.
D. PEDRO.   Good morrow, masters; put your torches out:
　The wolves have prey'd; and look, the gentle day,
　Before the wheels of Phœbus, round about
　Dapples the drowsy east with spots of grey.
　Thanks to you all, and leave us: fare you well.
CLAUD.   Good morrow, masters: each his several way.
D. PEDRO.   Come, let us hence, and put on other weeds;
　And then to Leonato's we will go.
CLAUD.   And Hymen now with luckier issue speed's
　Than this for whom we render'd up this woe.   [Exeunt.]

---

[1] guerdon] reward, recompense.

Scene IV. *A room in* Leonato's *house*.

Enter Leonato, Antonio, Benedick, Beatrice, Margaret, Ursula, Friar Francis, *and* Hero.

Friar.   Did I not tell you she was innocent?
Leon.   So are the prince and Claudio, who accused her
　　Upon the error that you heard debated:
　　But Margaret was in some fault for this,
　　Although against her will, as it appears
　　In the true course of all the question.
Ant.   Well, I am glad that all things sort so well.
Bene.   And so am I, being else by faith enforced
　　To call young Claudio to a reckoning for it.
Leon.   Well, daughter, and you gentlewomen all,
　　Withdraw into a chamber by yourselves,
　　And when I send for you, come hither mask'd.

　　　　　　　　　　　　　　　　[*Exeunt* Ladies.]

　　The prince and Claudio promised by this hour
　　To visit me. You know your office, brother:
　　You must be father to your brother's daughter,
　　And give her to young Claudio.
Ant.   Which I will do with confirm'd countenance.
Bene.   Friar, I must entreat your pains, I think.
Friar.   To do what, signior?
Bene.   To bind me, or undo me; one of them.
　　Signior Leonato, truth it is, good signior,
　　Your niece regards me with an eye of favour.
Leon.   That eye my daughter lent her: 'tis most true.
Bene.   And I do with an eye of love requite her.
Leon.   The sight whereof I think you had from me,
　　From Claudio, and the prince: but what's your will?
Bene.   Your answer, sir, is enigmatical:
　　But, for my will, my will is, your good will

> May stand with ours, this day to be conjoin'd
> In the state of honourable marriage:
> In which, good friar, I shall desire your help.

LEON.   My heart is with your liking.

FRIAR.   And my help.

> Here comes the prince and Claudio.

Enter DON PEDRO *and* CLAUDIO, *and two or three others*.

D. PEDRO.   Good morrow to this fair assembly.

LEON.   Good morrow, prince; good morrow, Claudio:
> We here attend you. Are you yet determined
> To-day to marry with my brother's daughter?

CLAUD.   I'll hold my mind, were she an Ethiope.

LEON.   Call her forth, brother; here's the friar ready.

[Exit ANTONIO.]

D. PEDRO.   Good morrow, Benedick. Why, what's the matter,
> That you have such a February face,
> So full of frost, of storm, and cloudiness?

CLAUD.   I think he thinks upon the savage bull.
> Tush, fear not, man; we'll tip thy horns with gold,
> And all Europa shall rejoice at thee;
> As once Europa did at lusty Jove,
> When he would play the noble beast in love.

BENE.   Bull Jove, sir, had an amiable low;
> And some such strange bull leap'd your father's cow,
> And got a calf in that same noble feat
> Much like to you, for you have just his bleat.

CLAUD.   For this I owe you: here comes other reckonings.

Re-enter ANTONIO, *with the* Ladies *masked*.

> Which is the lady I must seize upon?

ANT.   This same is she, and I do give you her.

CLAUD.   Why, then she's mine. Sweet, let me see your face.

LEON.   No, that you shall not, till you take her hand
> Before this friar, and swear to marry her.

CLAUD.   Give me your hand: before this holy friar,
> I am your husband, if you like of me.

HERO.   And when I lived, I was your other wife: [*Unmasking.*]
   And when you loved, you were my other husband.
CLAUD.   Another Hero!
HERO.   Nothing certainer:
   One Hero died defiled; but I do live,
   And surely as I live, I am a maid.
D. PEDRO.   The former Hero! Hero that is dead!
LEON.   She died, my lord, but whiles her slander lived.
FRIAR.   All this amazement can I qualify;
   When after that the holy rites are ended,
   I'll tell you largely of fair Hero's death:
   Meantime let wonder seem familiar,
   And to the chapel let us presently.
BENE.   Soft and fair, friar. Which is Beatrice?
BEAT.   [*Unmasking*] I answer to that name. What is your will?
BENE.   Do not you love me?
BEAT.   Why, no; no more than reason.
BENE.   Why, then your uncle, and the prince, and Claudio
   Have been deceived; they swore you did.
BEAT.   Do not you love me?
BENE.   Troth, no; no more than reason.
BEAT.   Why, then my cousin, Margaret, and Ursula
   Are much deceived; for they did swear you did.
BENE.   They swore that you were almost sick for me.
BEAT.   They swore that you were well-nigh dead for me.
BENE.   'Tis no such matter. Then you do not love me?
BEAT.   No, truly, but in friendly recompence.
LEON.   Come, cousin, I am sure you love the gentleman.
CLAUD.   And I'll be sworn upon't that he loves her;
   For here's a paper, written in his hand,
   A halting sonnet of his own pure brain,
   Fashion'd to Beatrice.
HERO.   And here's another,
   Writ in my cousin's hand, stolen from her pocket,
   Containing her affection unto Benedick.
BENE.   A miracle! here's our own hands against our hearts. Come, I
   will have thee; but, by this light, I take thee for pity.
BEAT.   I would not deny you; but, by this good day, I yield upon great

persuasion; and partly to save your life, for I was told you were in a consumption.

BENE.   Peace! I will stop your mouth.   [*Kissing her.*]

D. PEDRO.   How dost thou, Benedick, the married man?

BENE.   I'll tell thee what, prince; a college of wit-crackers cannot flout me out of my humour. Dost thou think I care for a satire or an epigram? No: if a man will be beaten with brains, a' shall wear nothing handsome about him. In brief, since I do purpose to marry, I will think nothing to any purpose that the world can say against it; and therefore never flout at me for what I have said against it; for man is a giddy thing, and this is my conclusion. For thy part, Claudio, I did think to have beaten thee; but in that thou art like to be my kinsman, live unbruised, and love my cousin.

CLAUD.   I had well hoped thou wouldst have denied Beatrice, that I might have cudgelled thee out of thy single life, to make thee a double-dealer; which, out of question, thou wilt be, if my cousin do not look exceeding narrowly to thee.

BENE.   Come, come, we are friends: let's have a dance ere we are married, that we may lighten our own hearts, and our wives' heels.

LEON.   We'll have dancing afterward.

BENE.   First, of my word; therefore play, music. Prince, thou art sad; get thee a wife, get thee a wife: there is no staff more reverend than one tipped with horn.

Enter a Messenger.

MESS.   My lord, your brother John is ta'en in flight,
    And brought with armed men back to Messina.

BENE.   Think not on him till to-morrow: I'll devise thee brave punish-ments for him. Strike up, pipers.   [*Dance.*]
                                                          [*Exeunt.*]

DOVER·THRIFT·EDITIONS

PLAYS